I0584593

In the Line of Fire

In the Line
of Fire

By Bryan M. Powell

Fantasy - Fiction, Christian - Fiction, Young Adult – Fiction,
– Fiction
Cover design by Bryan M. Powell
Photography by Photography by McCarthy

Manufactured in the United States of America
ISBN- 13— 979-8-9934312-5-3
ISBN- 10 –

Cast of Characters

Trace O'Reilly – As a private investigator, he begins to build a new career and life, but circumstances involving Lily and her key keep his life anything but normal.

Lily Peterson – Twenty-one year old millionaire, Lily tries to put the nightmare of Dr. Peterson behind her, but some ghosts cast long shadows.

Antonio Beretta – As the only living son of Luciano, he finds being the head of the Beretta crime syndicate more than he can handle.

Governor Sanchez – As a presidential candidate, he finds the pressure of being in the spotlight overwhelming. He has too many secrets, too many skeletons.

Cami Stetson – Candidate Sanchez's spokeswoman and close confidant with Trace, but is troubled with current developments.

Guillermo Jose Miguel Sanchez – The adopted nephew of the governor with no clear documentation of his birth.

Prologue

The silence of the afternoon was shattered by the crisp report from the .30-06 Winchester hunting rifle … the one Nelson Peterson used to take a shot at Governor Sanchez several weeks ago.

He kicked himself for not sighting it in earlier that day, a mistake he would not make again.

Peering through the scope, he cursed. No wonder he'd missed: The sights were way off. After making a few adjustments, he fired three times in quick succession.

Success.

Three shots … one hole in the center mass of the black silhouette target.

He smiled to himself and ratcheted back on the lever and jammed another shell into the chamber. Then, he took a steadying breath, released it and squeezed off another shot.

A perfect headshot.

With continued practice, he would be able to take out anything, or anyone at five hundred yards. Not that he would need to be that far away. But better to be prepared. Soon, whoever he got in his crosshairs would die a quick and bloody death.

No one took a picture of his Lily.

No one.

Since his narrow escape through the police roadblocks, he'd taken refuge in the deserted mountains east of Sacramento. It had always been his plan to bring Lily to his secret hideout. Years earlier, after his release from prison, he'd begged, borrowed and nearly stolen from his brother, Nate, to gather enough funds to build a modest cabin along the shore of a secluded lake. The pristine setting would have made Lily very happy. But he held out hope that one day his luck would change.

He sighed heavily at the missed opportunities. First, it was at the ski lodge. That ended in disaster and nearly got him killed. Then there was his latest attempt when he snatched her from the clutches of Beretta's thugs. Had it not been for her having a ruptured appendix, they would be living happily ever after, but no … that too ended in failure. Next time he would not fail.

And there would be a next time.

He just had to wait.

Chapter One

It had been over three weeks since Lily's ordeal with Dr. Peterson, and still her nightmares had not subsided.

His surgical skill, though often misapplied, was on par with the best. He'd successfully removed her appendix, leaving only four small incisions which, over time would heal nicely. She would be back in a bikini in no time.

I smiled at the thought.

With this new development, the doctors at Mercy General Hospital along with her personal physician and Dr. Kavani agreed the best course of action would be for Lily to continue her treatments locally rather than subject her to the rigors of international travel.

The plan pleased both Lily and me.

After my run with Wag, I was more than ready for a shower and to get started with my day. Unfortunately, with all my attention focused on saving Lily and helping her convalesce, my private investigator agency had suffered.

Not thinking, I tossed my keys on the counter. Lily jumped. Hand to her chest, she peered at me.

"Sorry, I didn't realize you didn't see me come in. How do you feel?" I came around the counter where she was sitting, leaned down and kissed her on the forehead.

"Shoo, you're sweaty," she said, squirming from my grasp. "Actually, I'm feeling tons better, but I have to say, I hate my doctor." Her nose wrinkled. "Can I say that?"

I stepped back, sniffed my sweatshirt disapprovingly. "Well, hate is a mighty strong word."

"Yeah, but he abducted me. I can't imagine what he might have done had my appendix not ruptured."

I had to agree. God was certainly watching out for her. I tried to lighten the mood. "One thing you can say about Dr. Peterson, he's not going to send you a bill for his services."

My statement brought a smile to Lily's face.

"I don't think he'll be bothering me anymore. From what I hear, he's on the FBI's most-wanted list. His face is in every post office from here to the Mississippi."

"Yeah, but who goes to the post office anymore?"

"Good point."

Her statement revealed an underlying belief that Nelson Peterson would never really be out of her thoughts, out of her life. Not until he was dead and buried.

Maybe never.

I hated that.

Lily swallowed hard, and her eyes rimmed with tears. "You know he saved my life, don't you?"

It was true, but the idea that he had touched my daughter made my blood run hot. "Actually, he was the one who ran Beretta's men off the road when they were chasing you."

Her face blanched. "I remember him saying something about that. I guess I should be grateful for small blessings. Maybe he wasn't trying to kill me after all. Maybe he really did love me in some sick sort of way."

She silenced me with a touch. "That man said something … something that got me thinking."

I waited.

"He said, 'These hands can save a life as well as take one.' Then he glanced down at me. His eyes glistened with emotion, and his voice trembled as he spoke. He said, 'I couldn't save your brother, but I'm going to save you.' Then he leaned over and kissed me on the forehead. Daddy, what did he mean?"

Like a phantom from the past, a shadow of hate, regret, guilt arose and scraped its claws across my memory. "I, I, don't know Honey. Those days are such a blur."

"Daddy, I remember you told me I had a brother, can't you tell me anything else?" Her pleas touched a place in my heart I thought I'd sufficiently sealed off.

My hands slicked. It seemed like years ago since we had that discussion. "Yes, not an identical twin, but yes, you have a twin brother. But your mother—"

Lily placed her hand on my forearm and squeezed. "Is Willie really my brother's name?"

My wet eyes met hers. I nodded. "Yes, but—" I had no answer to her questions … at least none she wanted to hear.

She shrugged. "I'm sorry I brought it up." She closed the Bible she'd been reading and stood.

It was encouraging to see her growing interest in the Bible, but I knew if I said anything, she'd clam up.

So I didn't.

"How 'bout you? Are you feeling better?"

I flexed my shoulder muscles, still stiff from the accident I'd had with Jimmy's truck. "I'm getting there. Running with Wag every morning is helping." Looking at the flowers and the card on the counter, I asked, "Troy bring these?"

Lily released a weak chuckle. "Yes, he just left a few minutes before you came in, I'm surprised you didn't see him."

I didn't.

"He said he had a lot of paperwork to do, that he'd come back as soon as he got through. Seems like even when I'm convalescing, I'm playing second fiddle to his career."

"Sounds like Troy."

"Sounds like you."

"Hey, I'm here as long as you need me. Truth is, he reminds me of me back in the day."

She shifted to face me. "Question, do you believe everything in this?" pointing to the Bible.

I had to admit, there were parts that I didn't understand, but I took it by faith.

"Yes, why?"

She fingered the cover. "I don't know. I was reading about that woman caught in adultery. According to the law, she should have been stoned, but Jesus told the men accusing her, he who is without sin, to throw the first stone."

I knew the passage well. "And one by one, they departed," finishing the passage. "So what's your question?"

Her face told me it wasn't just one question. It was many questions.

That was good. It was a starting point.

Sighing, she tapped her fingernail lightly on its leather surface. "I don't know, maybe we shouldn't talk about it. Right now, I need to clean up." She finger combed her hair. "I could sure use a shower."

My shoulders sagged, but I stayed upbeat. "Yeah," I chuckled lightly, "me too."

She turned to leave, but stopped. Touching the necklace, she said, "Daddy, have you gotten a good look at this?" she held it away from her neck.

"Honey, that necklace has been the bane of my life."

"I know, but could you take a look at it? Please."

I couldn't resist when her eyes bore into me. She looked so innocent, so childlike.

"Okay, you know there are people out there who would pay millions of dollars to get their hands on it."

"Yeah, but take a look at it. Have you noticed it's only half a key? I have the L side. But in order for it to unlock anything, I've got to get the other half, the part with the W."

I didn't want to encourage her. I knew the risks involved. It was just too dangerous.

She extended her hand, fingers wrapped tightly around an object. One by one, the digits relaxed until her hand was open. "Do you recognize this?"

"No, should I?"

She shrugged. "Mr. Observant, didn't you notice the earrings mother was wearing the night she was—" her voice trailed off.

"All I remember from that night was that she was wearing …" I felt my heart quicken. "Of course, she was wearing a pair of earrings, this being one of them."

"Exactly."

"And where did you get it?"

"You'll never believe it."

"Try me."

Lily shifted uncomfortably at the memory. "In Antonio's bedroom. When Mr. Carnes came to rescue me, I caught a glimpse of it and picked it up. Whoever killed mom must have brought her there before—"

"Before killing her," I finished the statement for her.

She nodded sullenly.

Squinting to get a closer look at the necklace, Lily turned it over in her fingers. "Mr. Carnes said something rather interesting just before we escaped."

I waited, not prodding.

"He told me Antonio wants this because he thinks it is a valuable piece of jewelry, but that Mr. Sanchez is the one who really knows its secret. Don't you have even the slightest tinge of curiosity about what secrets this key holds? After all, it was the cause of mother's death, and it nearly got me killed retrieving it."

She was right. I was very interested, but at what cost?

Chapter Two

After being pampered for weeks, Lily had enough. It was time to move on, and that meant getting answers.

With her second semester about to begin, she had just a few weeks to ferret out a mystery which had bugged her since the necklace had come into her possession. Dressed in a light-weight sundress, sandals and a broad-brimmed hat, she skipped from her condo and made her way to the parking deck.

The security detail she'd hired kept constant vigil over her. With precision, they shadowed her every move. They knew her itinerary, where she was going, who she talked to and when she would return. It was a small price to pay for peace of mind. And with a million dollar nest egg growing exponentially, she figured she could spend a little of it. The self-protection class she'd been taking provided an extra level of confidence in the event she was caught alone.

Today, she would go for a drive in her new Infiniti Q60 Coupe. The one her insurance company offered her was a shadow of the one she'd wrecked. So after hiring an attorney who made a living from suing insurance companies, they came back with a much better offer.

The two-car caravan crawled from the parking lot and

joined traffic. Her first destination was to the cemetery where her mother was interred. It had been a year since her last visit and despite her promise never to return, her heart yearned to go there one more time. The mums she'd picked up at the corner flower shop contained a mix of autumn colors. Not that her mother would have cared; it just seemed right.

Kneeling next to her mother's grave, Lily glanced around nervously. With her protective detail giving her space, she felt exposed, as if someone was watching her. She shook off the feeling and focused on the dash between the two dates. It was too short, then again, so was her mother's life. She just hoped her life would be a lot longer and more productive.

"Hello, Mom. I know it's been a while, but I've been busy." After recapping her year, she stopped. The feeling of being watched grew and she fingered the can of pepper spray which was her constant companion. "Mother, you used me." She spat the words out. "I know that now. The night you were killed, you had me dressed so men looked at me, wanted me. Was that your plan all along … to get them to—" She refused to let her mind sink to those depths. "Those pictures you had that man take, was that part of your twisted plan too? You were using me as bait.

"But they never touched me, I made sure of that. Not that you cared. You just wanted to get some dirt on those men so you could blackmail them like you did Sanchez. I feel so dirty. Why mother? Why did you have to defile everything you touched, including me? There's a lot of things I can forgive you for, but this—" her bitter sobs morphed into curses as she vented years of pent-up anger.

Anger at her mother, anger at herself. Finally, she stood.

"Why didn't you tell me I had a brother? I know you had your secrets and probably for good reason, but couldn't you at least have trusted me with one of them?" The pressure behind her eyes gave way and bitter tears scalded her cheeks. She wiped them away angrily. In the silence of waiting, she realized there were no answers here, only questions with no resolution.

With her hand on the headstone for support, Lily steadied herself and waited until she regained her equilibrium. "Well, I gotta go. I don't know when I'll be back, if ever. Goodbye."

Turning, blinded by tears, she staggered to her car. In her haste, she'd forgotten to leave the flowers. Frustrated, she tossed them aside and sped off.

***

She hoped her next destination would prove more productive.

At least her subject of inquiry was alive. Rounding the corner, a bubble of pride rose in her chest. Integrity Investigative Services was as much hers as her father's. Maybe the crimes he solves will leave a lasting mark on society for good. That way, her money, her investment would have been put to good use.

After parking, she waved back her detail. This was as safe a place as any and she would rather not drag them into the middle of what might turn out to be an uncomfortable situation. Anyway, this was her dad. They didn't need to protect her from him.

She did, however, have mixed feelings about bringing up the subject of her brother again, but she had to know, and he was the only one who knew anything about it.

Stepping into the impressive foyer, she breathed in the new paint and carpet smell. It smelled like a million bucks, she thought, or at least several hundred thousand.

After giving Cami a friendly hug and a brief explanation as to why she was there, Lily waited until her dad finished a phone call. Once the green light on his phone went blank, Cami gave her an encouraging nod and Lily stepped into her dad's office.

***

The door to my office opened slowly and Lily poked her head inside.

I just finished jotting down a few notes from my previous phone call and looked up. "Good morning."

Lily sauntered over, perching a hip on the corner of my desk, and offered me a disarming smile. "Morning to you. I didn't hear you leave."

Leaning back, I studied my daughter. "You were asleep and I didn't want to wake you. I had several things to do before I got here and grabbed a quick bite on the way in."

She eyed me narrowly. "We've talked about your quick bites. They usually involve a box of donuts or a bacon, egg and cheese biscuit."

Hands raised in surrender. "Guilty as charged. But seriously, I was running down a lead and needed to get a head start on the day. Now I suspect you didn't come here to chide me about my dietary proclivities. What can I do for you?"

Lily plopped into one of the deeply cushioned chairs. "Second semester begins in a couple of weeks, and I have a few things I'd like to get settled."

Leaning forward I placed my elbows on the desk and waited. I knew not to push her. She would say whatever was on her mind when she was good and ready.

"So, tell me about the night Willie and I were born."

I knew one day I'd have to have this conversation. It's like an adopted child wanting to find their birth parent. Only this time it was a twin wanting to find her other half. I wondered what it must be like to have another person think the same way, to feel things the same way, to be emotionally connected so that you only felt complete when you were together.

That was my Lily … that had to be Willie.

Her request couldn't be denied. I owed her an explanation or at least as much as I knew. Standing, I came around my desk and took the seat next to her. With my arms resting on my knees, I began, "Lily, you don't really want to know, do you?"

"Yes, I really do. I feel like something's missing in my life. I always have. It's just that I never knew what it was. Now that I do, I want to know more."

The front door swung open and Jimmy strode in, interrupting us.

"I tried to stop him, but he wouldn't listen," Cami said, apologetically, brushing past him and taking up a position next to Lily.

Lily stood. "Maybe I should go."

I reached out and stopped her. "It's okay Lily," giving her a quick glance. "Thanks, Cami, I'll handle it from here."

She shot Jimmy an angular look and stomped out. The door closed unusually hard, and I chuckled.

"Looks like you succeeded in making my secretary mad. Care to explain why you think you can bust into my office unannounced?"

Jimmy scanned the room and his eyes fell on Wag, who'd watched the scene unfold with passive interest. "Well, at least I didn't get your dog upset. Then I'd really have a problem."

"No kidding. Now why the interruption, Jimmy?"

The lines around his eyes deepened, and his smile faded. Taking a seat, he faced Lily, who was seated and peered at him suspiciously. "I hope you don't mind, but I followed you to the cemetery."

Lily sagged back. "I knew it. I knew someone was following me."

"Yeah, well, your protectors did a good job of keeping me at bay, but I have my ways of getting past them. I also know why you were there." Looking at me, he asked, "Do you mind if I answer her question? I was there, remember? But I have to say, it's going to be messy."

I held his steady gaze, then gave him a slow nod.

He leveled his gray eyes on Lily. "Your dad and mom had another fight. They fought regularly," shaking his head. "First it was over money, then it was his work schedule. That night it was over his drinking. He and I had been out all day on a nasty job and we both needed to decompress, so we went to our favorite watering hole. After a few drinks, I dropped him off at his house. Monica hit the ceiling." He paused. "Mind if I smoke," he asked, lighting a cigarette.

"Yes, now put it out," I said, my patience wearing thin.

He took a long drag, pinched out the ember and released a blue cloud. "If I remember right, she hit you."

I cringed at the memory.

Lily's eyes widened.

He continued, "Monica had a way of blowing things out of proportion, but I gotta tell ya, you said some pretty harsh things. You both did. Then she got in the car and sped off. The rest is in the police report."

"A police report!" Lily blurted.

Laying a hand on her wrist, Jimmy tried to calm her. "Yes, there was a police report. But I doubt you could find it. Anyway, she ran a red light, got broadsided, went into labor and nearly died." He ran his hand through his graying hair. "It was your Dr. Peterson, Monica's GYN, who saved her life and delivered you."

I leaned my elbows on my knees and took Lily's hand. This was not how I wanted her to learn this, and she wasn't handling it well. "If I remember right, the Doc was too inebriated to continue and had to be forcibly removed from the O.R. That I do remember."

Lily watched the exchange with growing concern. "But what about my brother? What about Willie?"

Jimmy inhaled and went into a coughing spell. When he finally recovered, he wiped his jaw with his sleeve.

"You all right?" I asked, handing him a bottle of cold

water I'd pulled from the refrigerator.

He fingered the stub. "Ah, these cigarettes are killing me. Doctor says I gotta quit or else." He took a swig and continued. "When Monica came out of recovery, Willie was gone, vanished into thin air."

Hand to her throat, Lily sucked in a sharp breath. "What happened to him?"

I looked at Lily. "At first, we thought it was Dr. Peterson, but couldn't prove it. Your mother blamed me, of course. She went into a deep depression, and I went on a three-week drunk. Our marriage sputtered along for a year or so. Then she served me with divorce papers. As a result, the police chief placed me on suspension. During all this time, the trail had gone cold."

Standing, I walked across the floor, faced the large pane window, and stared outside. An elderly woman wearing a red hat toddled past the window, unaware of my pain.

Jimmy cleared his throat. "Dr. Peterson was eventually cleared of baby-napping, but Monica sued him for malpractice. Got the guy five years." He stood and patted me on the shoulder.

I shook his hand off.

Jimmy retook his seat. With his eyes fixed on the horizon and picked up the story. "Some guy in Sacramento saw a picture of baby Willie on the news and connected the dots. Come to find out, Rafael Sanchez's first wife snatched the kid. Apparently, she was depressed over not having her own children. Willie happened to be an easy grab."

Blinking back her tears, Lily stood and wrapped her

arms around her waist. "If she took him, why couldn't you find him?"

Jimmy looked to me for the answer.

After taking my seat, I continued. "We couldn't, Honey. Mrs. Anna Sanchez overdosed on some sleeping pills and died before anyone could get a straight answer from her. Mind you, this took over six months to come out. By then, because of Dr. Peterson's incompetence and the hospital's negligence, all the records of Willie's existence had disappeared. To make matters worse, the state was unable to make a case against Mr. Sanchez. Your mother swore revenge, but that couldn't bring your brother back."

"Then we're no closer to the truth than before." She hiccupped out the words.

The line around Jimmy's eyes wrinkled. "Lily, I told you this would get messy. Truth is, you don't really want to know the truth. It's too ugly."

Lily's hands formed into two tight fists. "But I've got to know. It's important!"

Chapter Three

The moment Cami stormed in, Jimmy's mouth clamped shut.

Locking her gaze on him, she jabbed the air. "I don't know if you're here to ruin Governor Sanchez's reputation or derail his campaign, but whatever your reason, you need to leave … now!" She said unapologetically.

I'd never seen Cami so angry. Standing, I came around my desk and took her by the arm. "Cami, what's got you so upset? Lily has a right to know the truth."

Her eyes glistening, she stabbed Jimmy with a homicidal stare. "This better not screw up Lily's future. That's all I have to say." Turning, she slipped me a note, then stomped out of the office.

The others exchanged confused looks, but said nothing.

Once the air cleared, Jimmy eased himself onto the couch which Wag occupied. "All right, now where was I? Oh yes, I was about to tell Lily to sit down, and get a box of tissues, because this is going to hurt real bad."

Lily's mouth gaped as she retook her seat.

"Like I said, I was there, in the hospital, so was Luciano. I never knew Monica gave your brother a name." Taking out the stub of a cigarette, Jimmy fingered it longingly, then returned it to his pocket.

"What do you mean, Luciano was there?" I asked, my pulse quickening. "I don't remember that."

He gave me a sideways glance, crossed his arms and continued. "If you were there, you would have known. Before you and Monica hooked up, Luciano hired her to, uh, how should I say it, to entertain."

My jaw tightened. He'd already told me about him and Monica but apparently, he didn't bother to tell me everything. I hated for Lily to have to hear it. "You knew this and never told me?" my voice jacked up a notch.

Palms held in surrender, Jimmy backed away. "Hold on now buddy. I only recently learned some of this info. With me being persona non grata, and you behind bars, well, it just got lost in the shuffle."

Rubbing my chin, I released a tight breath. "Is there any other surprises you just happened to forget to tell me?"

Jimmy's face darkened. "There is one small thing."

I braced myself for what I assumed would be an avalanche.

"After your incarceration, I never stopped digging. You saw the notes I left my wife before my staged death."

I nodded, waiting.

"Well, those notes were just the tip of the iceberg. Like I said, Monica had her own little career going before you two got married. Occasionally, Luciano would set her up to entertain some of his wealthy clients. One such person was Mr. Rafael Edwardo Sanchez, who, at the time, was a budding star on the political horizon. After he got elected, she pressured him into giving her money to keep quiet." Shaking his head in unbelief, he cocked an eyebrow. "Can you believe it? The guy actually wrote her a check every month."

I leaned forward and placed my elbows on my knees. I knew Monica had Sanchez wrapped around her little finger. I just didn't know why.

Lily bravely fought back her tears.

With a smirk, Jimmy continued, "I got a photocopy of one of the checks. He'd written it for a hundred thousand dollars. And then there was that necklace with the key."

Lily bolted upright. "You mean Mr. Sanchez gave her that necklace? The one with the letter L on it?"

The crow's-feet around his eyes deepened. "No. Truth is, she stole it. I think she did it to remind Sanchez he owed her, big time."

The memory of her dangling it in front of everyone at dinner that night and making a toast to Luciano's generosity wafted across my mind.

Lily slumped back in her chair. "I tried to get her to give it back. I told her what I'd overheard about Santa Vern, but she wouldn't listen." Tears, mingled with black mascara, bled down her cheeks marring her otherwise beautiful appearance.

"You know why she married Attorney Nate Peterson, don't you?" Jimmy added candidly.

I shook my head. "No, why?"

"For his name," he said with a wet, hacking chuckle. After a moment, Jimmy regained control and continued. "She took his name just so she could worm her way into

Sanchez's election committee without his knowledge. She changed her hair color, had a few minor surgeries done to make her look years younger. Before you know it, she was back in business … the blackmailing business that is."

"And it got her killed," I added glumly.

Lily sagged into my arms, her shoulders heaving. "I knew she had all that done, but I thought she was just trying to—" her throat closed with another sob.

"I'm sorry, but I told you it would be painful." Jimmy didn't sound too remorseful. "Now, I gotta ask ya, where's the necklace?" Not taking his eyes off Lily.

She played with her ear mindlessly.

"It's somewhere safe," I answered before she could speak.

Lily pierced Jimmy with two fiery eyes. "So you're saying you are no closer to finding my brother than you were the day he went missing … just that Mr. Sanchez and my mom were," she paused and swiped a tear from her upper lip, "were somehow connected." She took a ragged breath and forced the next question from her mind. "Is the governor my real father?"

The question cut me to bone deep. "No, Honey, there is no mistaking the fact that you are my daughter." My lower lip trembled.

The atmosphere became electrified. After a moment, Jimmy scooted his chair back and stood. "I think I've done all the damage I can do for the time being. I need a rest."

My head snapped around. "You going somewhere?"

A distant gaze filled Jimmy's eyes, and he nodded

slowly. "I need a vacation. Maybe I'll visit my wife's grave, maybe I'll just disappear for a while. Seems like you got things pretty much under control here." His voice trailed off.

His abrupt change of demeanor concerned me, but I kept my mouth shut. I knew pushing Jimmy for more information would get me nowhere. I stood and walked him to the door. "I have only one question, before you go, Jimmy."

"Oh? Only one?"

I rubbed the back of my neck. "One for now, anyway. While your truck was impounded, I took the liberty to have your right rear tire scraped. We found traces of dog pee, which by the way, matched samples from a dog named Mitzi. Can you explain how it got there?"

A wily expression skittered across Jimmy's face and I knew he knew I was on to him. "Yeah, I can explain. I was there, at Mr. Horowitz's house, but I didn't kill him. Peterson did me the honor. Now I gotta go."

"It's not like you to give up on an investigation so easily, especially one that hits this close to home."

Jimmy shook my hand firmly. The years were wearing on him. "That's just it. It did hit home … my home. Now someone's going to pay," his eyes burned with determination.

He reached into his coat pocket and handed me a folded piece of paper. With a wink in Lily's direction, he said, "You've got a good man in Troy Ashcroft. Don't let him get away." Then he disappeared out the door.

From the window, I watched him get into his pickup truck and drive away. Part of me wanted to follow him, but I had a job to do, a hurting daughter to encourage and a lot of unanswered questions.

Unfolding the piece of paper he'd given me, I scanned it. It was ripped from an old newspaper and bore a date.

"What's wrong Daddy?" Lily asked, pulling my attention from the paper. "You look confused."

"I am. Jimmy just handed this to me." I refolded it and stuffed it in my coat pocket. "It's just another link in a long chain connecting Monica, Sanchez, and you and your brother. I don't know where it will lead. I don't even know if I can handle the truth when I find it." Looking at Lily, I released a long sigh. "I'm beat. How about you?"

Lily nodded absently and stood. "Maybe tomorrow will have more answers." She didn't sound convincing.

By the time we'd finished, Cami had gone for the day and the lights in the front office were dark. The note she'd slipped me earlier was curt. It said, *Don't trust a word he says.*

I didn't.

Chapter Four

The first brushstrokes of light spread across a cobalt sky awakening dozens of church bells throughout the Sacramento valley announcing another Sunday had arrived.

Lily wandered into the kitchen, dressed in a blue blouse, khaki skirt, and sandals. It was unusual for her to be up and dressed this early on a Sunday. Normally, she would sleep in, get a late brunch and chill out. Going to church was a new experience and I could tell she wasn't used to it.

"Are you ready?" I asked, laying aside my newspaper and looking over a pair of newly purchased glasses.

Lily gave me one of those looks. "You wouldn't want me to step out of this condo looking like I just rolled out of bed, now would you?"

I smiled. "No, Honey, you look great."

"Whatever."

"It's been a while since I've gone to church, and I'm kinda stoked about getting back in the habit."

She pinned me with a pair of cobalt pupils. "A habit? Get serious. I hope going to church isn't going to become a habit."

My heart dipped. I wanted to establish a routine of

church attendance, but calling it a habit was a poor choice of words.

"What I meant was—"

"I know what you meant. I just hope you don't want to drag me into your habit or routine or whatever. I'm not into that sort of thing, you know?"

Keeping my tone conversational, I tried another approach. "Well, for me, it's all about connecting with God."

She flipped her hair over her shoulder. "Whatever."

I stood, folded the newspaper and looked at Wag. "You stay off my chair, or I'll skin you when I get back."

Wag lowered his head and curled up on his pad.

After giving me an appreciative once-over, the corners of her lips curved up into a Mona Lisa smile. "You look snappy. I'd better stay close or some lonely widow is liable to snag you. Then I'll be out in the cold."

I tugged her close. "Ah, don't worry about me. Cami will see to that."

With her security detail off duty on Sunday, Lily skipped lightly down the stairs rather than take the elevator. I followed more slowly. By the time I'd gotten into her new car and clicked my seatbelt, she'd already started the engine and was revving it. I think she did it just to goad me.

"Don't you just love the smell of a new car?"

She inhaled. "It never gets old."

I figured with over a million dollars in the bank, she'll always have a new car.

Cocking her head, Lily asked, "Is Cami meeting us today?"

"No, not this week. The governor has her flitting all over the state setting up fundraisers and greasing the political wheels for his run for the presidency."

She was quiet the entire way to church and I wondered if her thoughts followed mine. I knew Cami. Since she'd become a believer, she'd become a woman of virtue, but I also knew what kind of man Sanchez was and I didn't trust him.

Lily shuddered as we entered the church parking lot. "From the little I know about Sanchez, I don't think I'm going to vote for him even if Cami works for him."

I returned her smile. "I don't blame you. I doubt even Cami will vote for him once she gets into the voting booth."

***

Sixty minutes later, I noticed her pensive mood.

"You're awfully quiet. Didn't you like the sermon?"

One of her shoulders inched up. "Oh, his delivery was cool and all. Not stuffy like most of the ministers on TV who read their eulogies or the ranting doom and gloom televangelists mom used to watch. My personal favorite was—"

"Lily."

"Whatever."

"You're using the typical evade and hide tactic."

She flipped her wrist as if swatting a fly. "Yeah, his sermon bothered me … a lot."

I glanced at the notes I'd scribbled on the back of the church bulletin. It happened to be from the same passage

Lily was reading the other day. The woman caught in adultery.

"So what's got you bothered?"

A long pause.

"Why would God want to hang out with a woman like that? I mean, it's not like He had to. Why her?"

I knew Lily was a deep thinker. This revealed a side of her I'd never seen, not that I'd seen that much of her. We were just now getting to the, 'speak to each other in a civil tone stage.' My probing into her spiritual psyche was above my pay-grade.

Being careful not to come across too harshly, I said, "I think in God's eyes, none of us are all that good. Take Nicademus for example. He was a priest. He was one of the good guys, and Jesus told him he needed to be born-again."

More silence.

She was thinking.

Not arguing.

That was good.

Lily blinked and touched the lobe of her ear. "I saw someone I thought I recognized, but I can't place his name."

Back to her evade and hide tactic.

I cringed, but said nothing. She'll open up when she is ready. Until then, I'll just have to wait and be a good listener.

I could do that.

"Was he nice looking?"

"No, it's not like that, I mean, yes. He was nice looking and all, but no, it's … it's so confusing."

I rubbed my forehead. "You got that right."

Lily stared at a distant object. "It's like he knew me. Like, maybe he was trying to remember my name. Then just as quickly, his face changed, and he stared right through me like I wasn't even there."

Instinctively, I reached over and took her hand. Her fingers intertwined with mine. "Well, if he were a real man, he wouldn't treat you like you were invisible. You can do better. By the way, what's with you and Troy?"

The air between us became tense, and I could tell I'd hit a raw nerve. She bit the edge of her lip. Finally, she brushed a few strands of sun-kissed hair behind her ear and sighed heavily. "Troy and I have been taking a break for a while. It seems like he wants things to move in a certain *direction,*" she formed air quotes, "that I'm not ready to go. Anyway, I've decided to really get serious with my classes in Criminal Justice." She let the words roll off her tongue as if she'd practiced them.

"Criminal Justice, hmm."

Bracing herself, Lily's shoulders grew rigid. "That's what Troy said, but remember, we agreed."

I blew out a breath. That was our agreement. We'd use her money to purchase the condo and get it furnished, and she'd put up the money for me to get my PI business started. And I would keep quiet about her pursuing a career in criminal justice. I'd secretly hoped she'd have developed an interest in other subjects. Like physics or biochemistry, or rocket science—anything but the rough and tumble business of law enforcement. I nodded slowly. "Well, if that's what you really want, then I'm all for it."

A nervous chuckle percolated in her throat, and she plunged into his arms. "Thanks, Daddy. That means a lot."

Chapter Five

" "What do you mean you went to a Baptist church in Sacramento?"

"You are not even supposed to be in California, let alone Sacramento." Governor Sanchez blistered the air between himself and his nephew. He had taken a long weekend off from campaigning to tie up some loose ends around his ranch. He didn't need or expect to find his nephew waiting to talk with him.

Gill stood, his shoulders squared, eyes fixed straight ahead. "But Uncle, you sent me to private Catholic schools my whole life. I was taught to go to mass every Sunday. It's sort of a habit I'd gotten into and thought I should go."

"But you said it wasn't a Catholic church. You said it was some kind of non-denominational, youth culture church."

"No, Uncle, I didn't say it was some youth culture church. I was running late, got lost and ended up in the parking lot of this big Baptist church. I went inside and found a lot of young people my age involved in leading the worship. A big difference from the stuffy old mass I'm used to."

The governor huffed. "That aside, why are you here in the first place? You're supposed to be in Boston attending classes at the Boston School of Law."

Clearing his throat, Gill jammed his hands in his pockets. "That's what I came to talk to you about. I've decided not to pursue a career in law. Rather, I want to study architecture, you know, be a builder. I want to build giant skyscrapers like the ones in New York City." His arms moved animatedly.

"An architect." Spit flew from the governor's lips as if he had blasphemed. "I didn't send you to the most prestigious schools in the country just to have you pouring concrete. I have big plans for you Gill, and it doesn't involve steel girders."

Governor Sanchez stood and began to pace. His heavy cowboy boots pounded out an uneven rhythm on the hardwood floor.

"Uncle, I appreciate all you've done for me. Really, I do. But I'm more of a hands-on sort of guy. I'm not cut out for courtroom drama or politics for that matter. I'm twenty-one. It's time I begin to make my own way in this world," his hands extended.

Sanchez always had a soft place in his heart for his nephew. He affectionately called him Gill, although his proper name was Guillermo Jos'e Miguel Sanchez. Over the years, he'd cast such a heavy shadow over the boy that he wondered if he would ever find his voice. Now he had.

Softening his tone, he stepped closer to his nephew, took him by the shoulder and leveled his gaze. "Son, all I've ever wanted is for you to have it easier than I did. God knows you didn't have it at the beginning. First, your parents died, then you were abandoned, left to fend for yourself on the streets of Sacramento. Were it not for the kindness of some stranger bringing you to my doorstep, who knows where you might have ended up."

It was all a lie, of course.

But Sanchez had repeated it so often, he'd come to believe it.

If only it were true.

If only Gill believed it.

And he had.

Guillermo was a tender, highly sensitive boy growing up. And his uncle took advantage of what he considered the boy's weaknesses. Using the power of persuasion, Sanchez instilled a deep sense of loyalty in his young protégée.

"Loyalty and Fidelity."

That was his motto, his mantra, his means of control.

And it was all about control.

His original plan was for Guillermo to become his right-hand man, to take up the mantle where he left off. But he could see Gill had other talents, other abilities. With a little push, he could be useful in other ways.

He pulled back and released a heavy sigh. "If this is what you really want, then I'll write a check to whatever school you choose."

"Uncle, you set up an educational fund for me years ago which I can use. Well, I'm ready. Cal State is planning on offering a school of architecture right in Sacramento. I could stay here and commute. That way, when I'm not studying, I could help out around the ranch. You know, get some hands-on experience."

Eyeing his nephew suspiciously, Sanchez retook his

seat and templed his fingers. He prided himself on his ability to read people, and right now he was getting all the wrong signals.

"Gill, my gut tells me there is more to it than you getting some hands-on experience."

The young man flopped into a wingback chair like a deflated balloon. A quizzical look covered his face. "I saw this girl—"

"Girl? What girl?"

Shifting uncomfortably, Gill straightened and leaned forward, resting his elbows on his knees. "The same girl I saw at Luciano's costume party; the one whose mother was murdered."

Sanchez's mind did a somersault back to that dark, rainy night. The same night in which Monica, wearing the necklace she'd stolen from him, was pushed down a flight of stairs. Gill had arrived unannounced claiming he was on holiday from school. Luciano insisted he get a picture of them.

A couple of hours later, the maid screamed and everything went to hell in a hand basket. Were it not for Luciano's quick thinking, he and Gill would have been embroiled in a controversy he couldn't afford.

"How do you know it was her? You know, that girl," the governor sputtered.

Gill's face brightened. "She looks the same, only more mature, grown up and all."

Pointing his index finger, Sanchez jabbed the air. "You stay away from her. She's trouble. Do you hear me?"

"But Uncle—"

"I said, stay away from her! Her mother tried to blackmail me and nearly sunk my run at the governor's office." His mouth snapped shut. Had he said too much? He hoped it was just enough to dissuade his gullible nephew not to investigate any further without raising his curiosity.

Gill jammed his hands into his pockets and prepared to leave. "I think she recognized me. I mean, for a moment, we looked at each other trying to remember something." He let an exasperated breath escape his lungs. "It's confusing." His voice trailed off, and he shook his head.

Sensing the young man's frustration, the governor stood and came around his desk. Patting Gill's shoulder, he guided him to the door.

"Look, Gill, I know this may sound harsh, but I gotta tell ya. The parents of that girl have given me untold grief, and she comes from the same stock. You need to put as much distance between you and her as possible. Understand?"

Gill's eyes widened. There was no reason to doubt his uncle. He had always believed him implicitly. He was like a father to him.

Loyalty and Fidelity.

Loyalty and Fidelity.

That was his motto.

But meeting this young lady had awakened his inner self. Though he couldn't put his finger on it, something stirred within him, an ember, a spark, a yearning ….

"I understand, Uncle. I'll stay focused on my studies, and make you proud," he said, his eyes unblinking.

Sanchez patted him on the back warmly and smiled. "You already have, son. You already have."

Sanchez retook his seat and watched Guillermo leave his office. Once the door closed, his smile faded into a sneer. Picking up the phone, he buzzed his secretary. "Millie, get Antonio Beretta on the line."

Chapter Six

❝Why are you calling me?"

Antonio Beretta hated to be interrupted in the middle of a private dinner with guests. Especially when it came from someone he looked at as a supplicant.

"You're the governor for Pete's sake. Can't you have one of your people handle it or are you too good to get your hands dirty?"

Pacing, Antonio stalked across the floor of the Beretta mansion like a mountain lion. He was used to calling the shots, not having some politician yanking his chain, expecting him to jump to his commands. The fact that his father and the governor went way back weighed little in his mind.

"This matter is a bit too sensitive for me to get involved," the governor said through pinched lips. "I can't have my name connected to it in the least or my chances of making a presidential run will go up in smoke. Plus, you owe me."

"Owe you? How do you figure that?" Antonio breathed heavily into the phone.

It was true.

The Beretta family owed Sanchez for its very existence. Were it not for him, the crime ring which permeated Sacramento would have been put behind bars years ago. "If we don't deal with little Miss Lily and that infernal necklace, we might be sharing a cell in San Quentin for a long time."

"You gave it to her mother in the first place, you fool. Why did you do it?"

Sanchez released a string of expletives. "I didn't give it to her. She stole it. And when that little snit daughter came looking for her it, you let her slip through your fingers. Now she has it and is asking a lot of questions. Questions I can't afford to have answered."

"Why did you have that blasted thing made in the first place?" Antonio was getting more agitated by the minute.

"I didn't. My wife did."

"You should have destroyed it, and any records associated with—"

"—Look, Antonio, it doesn't matter now. All that matters is that we get it back. If the press learns about it, I'm going down. You can be sure if I go down, so will you. Now get it back or you'll have the devil to pay."

The memory of that night replayed through Antonio's mind in stark imagery. Waking up with Monica Peterson's body lying next to him with her neck broken, her shocked expression, her eyes fixed on a distant horizon. The guilt of not knowing how she'd gotten there gnawed at his gut. His only recourse was to place the body at the bottom of the stairs and stage the accident. The only problem was Carnes, the maid, and Lily knew the truth. He didn't have to worry about Carnes and the maid. It was Lily who bothered him. Up until now, she'd kept her mouth shut. But with her asking a lot of questions, maybe it was time to silence her.

For a moment, the air between them grew tense. Finally, Antonio broke the wire-tight silence. "Okay, but this is the last time. After this, you're on your own."

Sanchez blew out a tight breath. "Yeah, until the next time one of your boys gets caught with a load of cocaine. Then it's 'Governor, can you do me a favor?'" His taunting voice echoed through the connection.

"So what do you want me to do with the girl?"

"I don't give a rat's rear end what you do with her. Just find that key and the jewelry box."

"Those two items could be anywhere. Do you have any idea where I should start looking?"

Sanchez huffed. "Do I have to do everything myself? How should I know? You might try asking your housekeeper. What's her name?"

"Rosa Tampico."

"Yes, Rosa. She was very close to—"

"—I know, I know. You've bemoaned it all before. I'll have my man question her. Maybe he can be more persuasive than I have. Got any ideas where to look for the necklace?"

"Yeah, you could start with O'Reilly's condo. If that doesn't work, try Lily's dorm room. From what I've heard, she never lets it out of her sight."

"Anything else? I mean, you're asking a lot."

A few seconds ticked.

"Yes, there is one other thing."

"And it is—"

"Put a tail on the girl. Let me know if she comes in contact with my nephew. I don't want those two to get together."

Chapter Seven

Standing outside his uncle's office, Guillermo listened.

His uncle needed him.

Loyalty and Fidelity.

Loyalty.

Fidelity.

He had never questioned those two words.

Never acted upon them.

Now was his chance to make his uncle proud.

His jaw set, he backed away from his uncle's door.

Find the necklace. Find the jewelry box.

Loyalty.

Fidelity.

Make Uncle proud.

***

Finding his former nanny wasn't such a big deal.

After all, she'd changed his diapers and watched him grow to an adolescent before Sanchez dismissed her. But she was never far away. Not physically, not emotionally. In a way, she was the one stable mother figure he had. When she went to work for the Beretta family, he'd kept in contact with her through texting and an occasional visit.

Today, sitting in the Beretta's kitchen, Guillermo felt right at home.

"How have you been?" she asked in her usual Spanish accent.

"I am fine Momma Rosa." He held her in a warm embrace. He could see the years in the service of the Beretta's had worn on her. The secrets, the backroom deals: even the bodies. She knew it all.

"You look good, Sonny. College suits you."

After placing a man-sized sandwich with chips and a pickle in front of him, she fisted her hips. "But not feed you like me."

Gill had to agree. He worked out at the gym regularly and had the biceps to prove it. He took several large bites and considered his nanny for a minute. He'd come seeking the answer to one question. And only she would know the answer.

He shoved the last bite in his mouth, chewed and washed it down with the sun tea, she'd proffered him.

"Rosa, can I ask you a question?"

The lines around her eyes creased. "Sonny, you are as close to me as anyone. Ask me anyting."

Guillermo dabbed his mouth and pressed ahead. "Do you remember anything about a jewelry box Aunt Anna gave you before she died?"

His memory of his aunt was sketchy. Only what Rosa told him. But one thing was memorable: the jewelry box.

Rosa stepped back, crossed her arms and studied him for a minute. "I knew one day you would ask me dat."

"You did?"

"Si, I mean, yes."

Her candor was refreshing.

She continued, "I remember da day when Miss Anna gave it to me as if it were today. She say, 'guard des with your life.'"

Mouth gaping, Guillermo couldn't hide his growing interest.

"What is in the box that is so important?"

Rosa shook her head. "I not know. She not give me da key. For a while, when I was still in da employ of your uncle, I kept it hidden in my closet. Then, when he dismissed me, I went to work for Luciano, God rest his soul," she crossed herself, "I took it to Father O'Leary. He is a good man. He promised me he would keep it until da time was right."

Guillermo drew his nanny into a crushing embrace. "I guess the time is right."

His next visit after class would be to St. Catherine's Catholic Church and, since it had been a while since he'd entered a confessional, it was time for a little of that too.

***

Dressed in a pink jogging outfit and wearing a pair of earbuds, Lily stepped from her dorm on the campus of the Cal State.

Eyes averted to avoid the bright sunlight; she skipped down the steps and turned right.

Thud!

She bounced off another student and landed on her backside. Frustrated and embarrassed, she picked herself up. A group of upperclassmen snickered as she stood and brushed off her bottom.

"Excuse me—"

A pair of piercing blue eyes stopped her mid-sentence.

Reaching down, he extended his hand. "I'm sorry, babe. I should have been watching where I was going."

Lily replaced one of the earbuds, which had fallen from her ear. "I'm not a babe. Dude!" Eyes narrowing, she asked, "Do I know you?"

His six-two frame towered over her. The action of him shaking his head allowed the sun to dance off his sun-bleached mane. He rubbed the three-day growth, which defined his strong jaw line. Flexing his biceps, he watched Lily's reaction and smiled.

"Uh, I don't think so," he muttered, scuffing the sidewalk.

His movements told her she made him nervous, but she had to know. "Didn't I see you at church Sunday?"

Hands held in surrender, he backed away. "Look, I didn't see you on Sunday or any other day. Stay away from me, do you hear?" He reversed his direction and jogged down Bay Laurel Way.

"Hey, wait," Lily called after him. Picking up his class schedule, she waved it in the air. "You forgot this."

"Forget it," he called over his shoulder and disappeared around a corner.

Lily huffed, wondering what just happened.

Chapter Eight

It wasn't hard to find Rosa Tampico.

All Giorgio Vincent had to do was to wait until her shift was over and follow her home. That was where he did his best work.

Alone.

Giorgio, a cheap thug, and veteran of the prison system, was Antonio's go-to guy. After years of carrying out his boss's dirty work, he'd come to believe he was untouchable. He was smart. Very smart.

His half shaven face, straggly hair and baggy clothes made him blend in with all the other street people. Even his bum knee worked to his advantage. People tended to ignore the indigent, ignorant and injured. To all but the most observant, he was the invisible man.

And tonight he wanted to be invisible.

"Good evening, Rosa."

Hand to her chest, she dropped the pan of refried beans she'd been carrying. "Where did you come from?" she gasped as she jumped back from the steaming pan.

Giorgio feigned an apology. "Sorry, if I frightened you. The door to your apartment was open and I was in the area and thought I'd check on you." The door certainly wasn't open, not until he'd picked the lock and let himself in.

"What do you want?" Rosa's voice had an edge to it.

He moved to his right, countering her move. An instant before her hand reached the butcher knife, his hand shot out and grabbed it. "Here, let me get this—wouldn't want you to cut yourself on it. Now would we?"

Rosa backed away. She'd never liked Giorgio. In her opinion, he came from the wrong side of the Rio Grande and she'd told him so on several occasions. Eyeing him with suspicion, Rosa moved to the opposite side of the room.

"Take a seat, Rosa. I have a few questions to ask you."

She resisted.

He lashed out, grabbed her and threw her into a wobbly wooden chair. Its legs creaked but held.

In a flash, Giorgio yanked the old-fashioned rotary phone from the wall, stripped off the cable and wrapped it around her.

She struggled and cursed.

He ignored it.

When he'd completed his task, he lightly bounced the butcher knife in his hand.

"Now I'm going to ask you a few questions and you're going to answer me truthfully. Understand?"

She glowered at him.

He forced her left hand from her crossed arms and flattened it on the kitchen table. In one swift move, he chopped off her little finger.

"Understand?" His voice was strained.

She ground out a labored, "Si."

"Good. I thought we could come to an

understanding."

Holding the independent digit, he said, "Question one, where is the key? You know the one?"

She bit her lip to keep from crying out. Shaking uncontrollably, she said, "I not know."

Another finger fell under the knife. It was the ring finger.

This time she released an ear-piercing scream.

He ignored her pleas for mercy.

Mercy was not in his vernacular.

Lifting the second newly freed finger, he asked, "Where is the jewelry box? I know you know."

Rosa did her best to control her breathing but despite her best effort, she started to hyperventilate.

By now, a current of bright, red blood streamed from Rosa's left hand, and she was shaking violently.

"The jewelry box," he demanded.

Releasing her hand, he grabbed a plastic grocery bag and pulled it over her head and tightened it with the remainder of the phone cord.

"By my calculations, you have about two minutes before you lose consciousness. Now tell me where the jewelry box is."

Despite her missing fingers, she clawed at the bag. She sucked in the remaining air, leaving a gruesome sight.

Moments before she passed out, she began a muffled prayer.

"Save your breath, sister. You're going to need it."

Her words became slurred, her head drooped. She was dying and Giorgio was no closer to his query.

As he turned to leave, she said one final name before expiring. "Father O'Leary."

"So you want Father O'Leary to pray for your soul? Hmm? Better yet, why don't I pay him a little visit? Maybe he can hold your hand while you two cross the great divide." He laughed at his cruel joke.

But first, he had a couple other visits to make. Rosa would just have to hang out in limbo until he could make other arrangements.

Chapter Nine

A white panel truck pulled to a stop in front of Trace's condo and a repairman jumped out.

After scanning the area for unwanted eyes, Giorgio opened the rear door and grabbed his toolkit. With practiced skill, he casually strolled around to the side of the condo unit and disconnected the alarm. Knowing he had only a few minutes before the owners were alerted, he arranged a little surprise. All it took was a small fender bender to delay Trace long enough for him to do the job.

Wearing a pair of rubber gloves, he unlocked the front door and stepped inside. As he turned, two large paws pounced upon his chest, pressing him against the door frame.

"Whoa, there boy, I'm just a friend looking in on you." Reaching into his pocket, he pulled out a plastic bag containing a T-bone steak. "Here, this should keep you occupied."

After placing the meat in Wag's food bowl, he stepped back. In an instant, the dog diverted his attention from him to the steak. Satisfied he'd rendered Wag useless as a guard dog, he quickly went to work.

First, he did a thorough search of Lily's room.

Nothing.

The rest of the condo yielded nothing either.

***

After her last class, Lily returned to her dorm only to find her door standing half open.

Her breath caught in her throat. Since she'd enrolled in college, she'd dismissed her security detail. Now she wished she hadn't. "I could have sworn I'd closed that door when I left," she muttered.

Hoping her witless roommate was the guilty party she pushed deeper into the room. "Mikala?" she called into the darkness.

No answer, but movement in her bedroom stopped her heart.

"Mikala, what are you doing in my bedroom." She'd asked her roommate to respect her privacy. Obviously, she'd not done so.

A shadow moved, and something heavy struck her from behind. Flashes of red and yellow splintered her vision. Her legs buckled and she toppled to the floor.

***

"What's that ringing?" Lily mumbled, trying to lift her head.

Squeezing her eyes shut, she felt the room sway like a pendulum. "Mikala?" she called. Her voice sounded distant.

A wave of panic washed over her. Had Nelson Peterson returned? Was her life in danger? Reaching for anything solid, her fingers found a chair and she pulled it closer. With some effort, she pulled herself to her feet. Dim light from outside filtered through the curtains revealing the damage done to her dorm. None of it made sense. This was her first week at college. Had she made an enemy? Or was this the typical hazing she had heard about?

On shaky legs, she walked over and flipped on the lights. Sucking in a sharp breath, her hand covered her mouth. Her flat-screen TV lay face down. Every drawer in the living room had been emptied; their contents lay strewn across the floor. Her bedroom wasn't much better. Her bed had been flipped over. Every garment she owned had been tossed around like some wild beast went on a rampage.

Anger welled in her chest at the thought of a stranger pilfering through her belongings. She thought about calling the campus police but didn't want to be labeled a troublemaker the first week of school. After all, it didn't look like anything was missing. Even her laptop and computer were where she had left them, albeit covered with her undies. Heat crept up her neck.

Picking up her cell phone, she hit the speed dial. "Trace." Her throat closed and she melted into tears.

"Honey, what's wrong?"

Lily took a halting breath. "Trace, someone ransacked my apartment," she hiccupped a sob. "I'm so scared. Are you sure—"

"Don't even think it. Peterson is gone." He didn't sound too convincing.

"Trace, is there something you're not telling me?"

She only called him that when she was really upset.

He released a heavy sigh. "I didn't want to worry you, but I got a call from the security company. Our condo has been broken into also. It doesn't look like they got anything. If it weren't for a stupid fender-bender, I would have caught the intruder red-handed. Looks like the guy was hunting for something, and when he didn't find it, he must have decided to pay your room a visit."

Lily's breath turned to ice—was he looking for her necklace?

Chapter Ten

Soft organ music played through the sound system giving the dimly illuminated sanctuary of St. Catherine's Catholic Church a warm, inviting atmosphere.

Father O'Leary, the elderly priest who presided over a small flock of parishioners, glided down the aisle. His black robes whispered softly as he passed the faithful.

"God bless you, my children," his voice was low, reverential.

Halfway down the aisle, he paused and laid his hand on the shoulder of a young college student's shoulder. It was unusual for the younger generation to come seeking God. It did his heart good.

"God bless you my son. You have done well to seek God while you still can."

Guillermo lifted his head. He had been praying for wisdom and direction. But his prayers didn't seem to be getting anywhere. Maybe Father O'Leary could help remedy that. He'd waited for over an hour in the dim sanctuary for the elderly man to show up. Now that he had, Guillermo felt his resolve weakening. Standing, he towered over the demure gentleman by at least a foot and a half.

"Padre, I was wondering if I might have a word with

you privately." He glanced around at the few who gathered for the Saturday night mass. Nobody paid him any attention.

That was good.

The elderly priest, always eager to help those in need, extended his hand to show him the way to his study.

Once inside, he offered him a seat. His study was nothing like his uncle's. As a matter of fact, it was just the opposite. His uncle's was lined with plaques, certificates, pictures of him and some famous celebrity or politician. Father O'Leary was the epitome of humility. It was something Guillermo wanted to emulate, but first he had to get his hands on a certain jewelry box.

Hopefully, the priest still had it.

Taking a seat behind a simple desk, Father O'Leary folded his hands as if praying and asked, "How can I help you, my son?"

His tender voice stood in stark contrast to that of his uncle's. It made him want to linger, but he had things to do.

"Before my mother passed, she entrusted a jewelry box to my nanny. Her name is Rosa Tampico—"

"Yes, Rosa. She is a very faithful member of my flock. I know her well."

That was encouraging.

"Yes, well, she was my nanny until I was about ten when she left my uncle's service and began to work for …" he paused, not wanting to divulge too much. "Anyway, she said she gave you the jewelry box for its safe keeping. I was wondering if you still have it."

The priest was on his feet nearly before Gill had

finished his question. Giving the closed door a quick glance, he swung aside a portrait of the current pope revealing a safe. He dialed the code and pulled open the door.

Speaking over his shoulder, he said, "She told me one day you would come asking about it. I have kept it safe all these years."

Sharp rapping interrupted their meeting.

"Please excuse me, my child."

Guillermo retook a seat.

A hushed conversation followed. Father O'Leary returned looking deeply moved.

"I'm sorry to have to end this, but, I just received word that Miss Rosa Tampico has just been found. Apparently, she's been murdered."

Guillermo's jaw fell open. "Murdered!" he repeated.

"Yes. I must go." Grabbing his tattered Bible and rosary, he made for the door.

***

Father O'Leary had only gone a few steps down the hall when a man sporting a dark trench coat and a hoodie materialized directly in front of him.

"Oh, excuse me," the priest said, glancing up as he adjusted his regalia. "I didn't see you. Is there something I can do for you?" Even though he was in a hurry, he took the time for one more stranger.

"Father, it's been a long time since I've been to confession. I was wondering if I might—"

"The Lord bless you, my son. It is never too late for

one of God's children to return to the fold."

Unseen by the priest, a cruel smile stretched across the intruder's face.

"I'm in a bit of a hurry, so let's just dispense with the usual catechism." As he spoke, he slipped into his side of the confessional. "Now, if you're ready—"

The muzzle of a silencer protruded through the velvet curtain and fired two shots in rapid succession. A soft gasp preceded the sound of the priest slumping forward, striking his head on the frame of the booth. Immediately, a pool of crimson blood formed a half circle under the door as the hooded man stepped out.

Silent as death, he slipped into the priest's chambers. The safe door hung open and the jewelry box was exactly where Father O'Leary left it. He snatched it up and stuffed it into his backpack. Only then did he realize Guillermo was sitting in a chair against the paneled wall, his eyes wide.

"What are you doing?" Guillermo's question caught him off guard.

Instinctively, he reached for his gun, but the silencer hung on the corner of his topcoat.

Seeing the weapon, Guillermo leapt upon the man. Between the trench coat, the weighted backpack and the snagged gun, Giorgio was at a disadvantage.

Guillermo grasped for the weapon, shoved him backward until he slammed against the bookcase. Theological books and study guides toppled to the floor. A moment later, the two men stumbled over the ancient tomes and fell one on top of the other.

Releasing a filthy oath, Giorgio stopped trying to pull

his gun out. He pulled his switchblade from his pocket and pressed the button. The six-inch blade sprang out. With the flick of his wrist, he brought it within a millimeter of Guillermo's jugular vein.

Guillermo pulled back and leveled an iron fist against Giorgio's jaw. The blade loosened in his grasp, but he retained control of the handle.

Using a street fighting technique he'd learned the hard way, Giorgio released a volley of punches to Guillermo's chest, head and gut leaving him spitting blood.

Giorgio was on his feet in an instant. He could kill this young man, but he was not getting paid to go on a killing spree. Instead, he sprang through the office door. Not being familiar with the layout of the church, Giorgio turned right and found himself in the main auditorium.

Too late to change directions.

One last glance over his shoulder and he dashed up the side aisle. Two rows from the back an elderly woman stepped directly into his path. Their eyes locked.

His breath chilled. *Should I kill her?*

No time.

Too many witnesses.

Not getting paid to go on a killing spree.

Giving the woman a slight nod, he skipped around her and dove through the exit.

She was still watching him.

***

It took less than fifteen minutes for the call to reach the

dispatcher and for Troy Ashcroft and the CID unit to arrive at the scene.

After doing a complete inspection of the confessional and the priest's office, he glanced around. Rubbing the back of his neck, he wondered why anyone would kill a priest. It made no sense. The man had taken a vow of poverty. He owned little. He lived a simple, humble life in service to God and mankind. His death seemed such a waste.

Troy pulled a pen from his shirt pocket, double clicked it and began to take notes. "Why would someone kill a priest in cold blood?" he muttered.

"What's that, sir?" One of his men asked.

Shaking his head, Troy glanced up from the sheet covered body. "Nothing. I was just thinking out loud." His eyes flitted around as he tried to reconstruct the last moments of Father O'Leary's life.

A bevy of activity continued as police and a team of forensic investigators began the methodical process of collecting evidence. Troy stepped away from the body and approached a college student.

"Are you the one who called us?"

Guillermo gulped. He'd never spoken to anyone in law enforcement—never had to. He nodded slowly.

"I need you to tell me everything you saw."

Badly shaken, he sniffed back a tear and began a detailed description of the evening's events. It surprised Troy the precision of Guillermo's statement. From the man's muscular build to the tattoo on his right forearm, he described his attacker in great detail.

"He wore green cargo pants, and he had on a pair of

black Nike's sports shoes, very expensive. Probably knockoffs," he muttered.

Satisfied, Troy thanked Guillermo and handed him his card. "Don't hesitate to call me if you remember anything else."

Guillermo nodded absently and headed back outside where his Jeep Renegade sat under a shade tree.

Chapter Eleven

I finished putting the final touches on a missing person's case and filed it away when my phone rang.

With Cami in full campaign mode and Lily taking classes, it left me with the job of answering the phone, filing and a myriad of other secretarial duties. It was a wonder I got any investigating done for all the menial tasks I had to perform. The last thought I had before snatching up the phone was, *I gotta hire a secretary.*

"Trace? Got a minute?"

I blew out a tight breath. At least it wasn't the parents of the missing child. Come to find out, the child in question was neither a child nor was he missing. His overly protective parents had sheltered the young man until and after he'd reached adulthood. Now that he was twenty-one, he thought he'd try out his new wings. I found him and his girlfriend enjoying a cozy weekend in the mountains.

"Hey Troy, what's up?" My mind was still on the love-birds in the mountains.

"Have you been watching the news?"

"No, why?"

Troy shifted the phone from one ear to the other by the sound of it. "We've got another murder. This time it's not one of Luciano's associates."

"Not one of Luciano's men, hmm? Who was it?"

This was the first murder since a string of murders took out most of Luciano's closest associates.

"I've got two back-to-back murders. With the department providing an extra layer of security for Sanchez we're a bit stretched. Mind lending us a hand?"

"Sure, where are you?"

"I'm at St. Catherine's Cathedral. It's the priest, Father O'Leary. He'd been shot twice at close range. Then his chambers were searched, and his safe was broken into."

"A priest? Why him?" He had my interest.

"Too early to tell."

"Any witnesses?"

"Yeah, a young man stumbled on the whole thing. Guy's name is a doozy."

"What is it?"

"It's Guillermo Jose Miguel. Goes by Gill."

The name meant nothing to me, but Troy sounded rattled. I knew he'd been trying to patch things up with Lily. I also knew she'd taken up residence at U. of C.'s campus in Sacramento to pursue a career in Criminal Justice. Although he'd made a valiant effort at dissuading her to go out with him, Lily's mind was made up.

Stubborn like me.

She had a nose for details.

She would make a good investigator.

"That's what I'd like to know—"

Troy's statement punctured my train of thought like a pin to a balloon. I caught myself scrambling to piece his fragmented statement together. "His chambers were also burglarized."

"Yeah, well, there's been a rash of that lately." I kept my voice level.

"What do you mean?"

"Oh, you haven't heard?"

"Heard what? Come on Trace, level with me."

I blew out a breath. "I didn't want to bother you with this. It's kinda out of your league now that you've made sergeant in the CID unit—"

"Trace!" His frustration sliced through the connection.

"Okay, okay. Truth is, both Lily's dorm and my condo were broken into. Nothing was taken to my knowledge, but they certainly made a mess of things."

"Broken into? I thought you had the state-of-the-art security system."

"Yeah, well, I do, or at least I thought I did. But then I found the remains of a T-bone steak in Wag's food bowl. This guy knew what he was doing. It probably took him less than fifteen minutes. Did the same thing to Lily's place only ..."

Troy swore under his breath. "Only what? Trace you are driving me nuts. Would you just say it?"

"All right, when Lily stepped into her dorm, she must have spooked the thief. The next thing she knew, she had a knot on her head the size of Mt. McKinley. So much for it being a panty-raid."

I could hear movement and could only guess that Troy was on his feet, pacing. "Is Lily going to be okay? I mean, did—"

"No, Troy, nothing like that. And it wasn't Nelson Peterson. I can assure you of that."

"How can you be so sure? He could be anywhere, just waiting for his chance to abduct her again."

"Troy, if it was him, well … trust me, it wasn't."

I wasn't so sure.

How could anyone be sure?

Nelson Peterson simply disappeared.

No trace. No trail. No leads.

He could be anywhere.

 And that was a problem …

"Did anyone get a look at the guy?"

"The campus police interviewed all the students on her floor, and nobody saw anything. He made a clean getaway."

"Can I see Lily?"

"She's shaken up a bit, but I think she's okay," which wasn't much of an answer. "I told her to move back in the condo, but since the thief got by Wag and the security system, she doesn't think she'd be any safer there. I told her to reactivate her protective detail, but …" I let my voice trail off. She is one stubborn girl.

"Did they get anything?" I heard Troy double-click his pen. An action I'd seen him do a dozen times.

 "That's what's got me puzzled. I think the thief was after the necklace. Fortunately, she was wearing it under her blouse. Since he didn't find it in my condo, he came after Lily."

Troy was quiet for a moment as he scribbled a few notes. "Look, Trace, would you mind coming on board for just a little while until we get a handle on this? I've got a bad feeling about this."

Another long pause.

This time it was my turn to ponder. "Troy, you know how the chief feels about me. He promised he'd reinstate me, then double-crossed me. That good for nothing, butt kissing—"

"Okay, Trace, you made your point. Will you do it for me?"

I huffed into the phone. "No, but I'll do it for Lily. I want to get my hands on the jerk who whacked her on the head, and throttle him."

Troy let out a nervous chuckle. "That might violate police protocol."

"To heck with police protocol. That's Lily we're talking about."

"I'm with ya, man. How about we meet at our usual dining establishment, and I'll go over what I've got."

"I'll be there in twenty minutes, depending on traffic," I said, holstering my 9mm and tugging on my sports coat.

Chapter Twelve

Having her dorm room trashed left Lily in a foul mood.

She tried to study, but it was useless. After sitting in the media center staring at a screen for hours, her fanny ached.

She needed a break. Unlike most libraries, the campus library at the university had its own version of Starbucks. Looking for a good reason to set her books aside, Lily stood, stretched and began to root through her purse for some loose change. After digging through every pocket, she finally scraped enough money together for a mug of coffee and a pastry. Although she had over a million dollars in the bank, she'd put herself on a strict budget and refused to touch the principle.

Her stomach growled. Glad there were no students close enough to hear, she made her way to the coffee shop adjacent to the library. Skipping breakfast wasn't such a good idea, she chided herself. Maybe a Grande will pick me up.

Smiling at the preppy nineteen-something girl with purple spiked hair standing behind the glass counter, Lily said, "I'll take a coffee Grande and a cranberry muffin."

After paying, she stood to the side and waited, hoping her stomach would quiet down. Hand on her mid-section, her mind wandered back a few months to her emergency surgery. *Maybe Nelson Peterson was just trying to save my life. Maybe he really cared for me.* She shook those thoughts from her head as her name was called.

The same purple haired girl set the tray with her order on the counter.

"Thanks," Lily said. Turning, she headed to her seat. The aroma of the freshly brewed coffee sent her stomach into overdrive. "Sugar, I forgot to get some packets of sugar and butter," she told herself and reversed direction.

Suddenly, a student with his nose in a book stepped into the aisle and collided with her, sending the muffin tumbling to the floor

"Well, excuse me!" Lily huffed, balancing the tray with one hand and brushing the hot coffee off her wrist with the other.

"I, I'm sorry. I didn't see you," the red faced young man sputtered, giving her an appreciative once-over.

Lily tucked the necklace, which had fallen out from under her sweatshirt, back into place. "If you didn't have your nose stuck in that book, you might have." Lily's voice cut through the silence.

"Shh," a lean bespectacled woman with her hair in a bun warned. She was probably the original librarian, Lily surmised.

Returning her attention to the guy towering over her, she caught herself staring into a pair of cobalt blue eyes. For a moment she thought she saw recognition in them, then it vanished.

"The least you could do is to offer to buy me another muffin and coffee."

"Oh, yes, how stupid of me," he said, patting his pockets. "Only, I left my wallet back in the dorm room. But not to worry," lifting his index finger. "I can use my campus card," he said, flashing both it, and a pearly white grin.

Lily's heart skipped a beat and she returned a weak smile. She hated using a credit card and the cavalier way he dealt with problem-solving irritated her. *He's probably some rich kid here on a football scholarship and hasn't worked a day in his life. Then again, I'm a rich kid who's never worked a day in my life, so what's the big deal?* "Okay, but I'm not accustomed to using credit." She blurted, then regretted it.

A blank expression spread over his face. Clearly, the concept of paying for his own expenses hadn't occurred to him. Leaning over, he picked up her crumbled muffin and glanced around for a trash can.

"Here, I'll take it," Lily said, rolling her eyes. She took it from him and tossed it in the trash. Then she collected her computer bag and followed him to the coffee shop. Disappointed that she'd ordered the last cranberry muffin, she sighed. "I guess I'll settle for the blueberry one," she said to the confused purple-haired girl behind the counter.

"Make that two and two pumpkin spice Lattes with cinnamon."

Lily glared at him. "I was going to order another Grande. Anyway, what kind of guy drinks a pumpkin spice Latte with cinnamon?"

Unmoved, Gill shrugged off her comment and handed the purple-haired girl his card. "Just put it on my account," he said with a wink and a wolfish grin.

The color of the girl's face went from powder white to a deep shade of pink. Fanning herself, she turned away to fill the order.

Great, is this guy a trip or what? Lily tried to ignore the knot in her stomach. *Does he do that to every girl he meets?* Her thoughts fluttered like moths around a flame. She was both drawn and repulsed.

Intrigued, she followed him to an empty booth and took a seat. It suddenly occurred to her that she needed to breathe. *What is wrong with me? He's just a guy and anyway ... he's not my type. So why can't I stop staring at him?*

In an attempt to break the moment, she focused on a sign which hung on a billboard announcing the formulation of an anti-government protest. *Great, I love the smell of tear gas in the morning.*

"So, what are you majoring in?" She knew it was a dumb question, but it was the first thing that popped out of her mouth.

The guy smiled at a passing co-ed, then returned his attention to Lily. "Uh, what did you say?"

"Never mind, I think I know the answer." Standing, Lily started to turn when a strong hand grabbed her by the wrist. "Hey, don't go, you haven't got your order."

Lily glanced down at his hand. It was scratched and red like he'd been punching a brick wall. "If you don't let me go I'll have to break your arm."

His grip loosened. He flashed a heart-stopping smile. "Oh, sorry. I didn't mean to come on so strong. I witnessed a—" His voice trailed off.

"You witnessed a what?" Lily's interest piqued.

His muscular shoulders slumped. "I, I, I caught a man breaking into Father O'Leary's study at the Catholic church, after he killed him and I'm, well, a bit shaken up."

He pulled in an unsteady breath and looked away. "He didn't see me in Father O'Leary's study. When I asked what he was doing, he tried to pull his gun, but it got tangled in his coat. For a second, I thought I was a dead man. All I knew to do was go for his throat, man. I nearly had him, but he landed a couple of good punches and got away."

Eyes widening, Lily's heart softened. "So that explains your knuckles."

The young man glanced at them, then pulled his hands back and hid them under the table."

Shifting the conversation, he asked, "What's your name."

Lily's skin tingled. Looking into his eyes, she felt her world tilt. Catching her breath, she retook her seat. "My name is Lily Peterson, but I hate my last name. I'm thinking about changing it."

"Changing it? Changing it to what?"

Lily's heart slammed against her ribcage. "To O'Reilly."

For a moment, the young man held her gaze. "O'Reilly ... are you Irish? You don't look Irish."

"I may not, but my dad is," she said, though she didn't know to what percent.

His lips moved as he repeated the name. "O'Reilly, O'Reilly. That's funny. For some reason, I seemed to have heard that name before, but I just can't place it. Of course, like mine, there's probably hundreds of O'Reilly's in Sacramento." He blinked away his confused expression.

On cue, Lily asked, "So what's your name?"

Giving her a disarming smile, he fingered the charge receipt. "It's Guillermo."

Hand to mouth, Lily stifled a grin. "What kind of name is that?"

His face reddening, he ran his fingers through his thick, rakish hair which ended just below his earlobes. Giving the nape of his neck one final rub, he sighed, "Well, my full name is Guillermo Jose Miguel Sanchez, but my friends call me Gill." He offered her his best smile, the kind which stopped her breathing, her heart and blew out the circuits in her brain.

"You don't look like a Gill," she sputtered.

Feigning offense, he leaned back. "So what do you think I look like?"

Finger to her chin, Lily searched the ceiling. "You look like a Richard, or a William."

Gill let out a tight breath, and his smile slipped slightly. "Actually, the English pronunciation of my name is—"

Suddenly, the tune by Jason Aldean's *Burnin' It Down* stole his attention, and he looked at his cell phone. "Hold that thought," he said, his finger raised.

While he carried on a one-sided conversation, Lily doodled on the paper napkin. *Probably some dumb blond bimbo,* she surmised. *Wait, I'm a blond, now anyway. Maybe I should color my hair ... black, yes black. No one's ever made a movie about being Legally Black.*

The conversation ended and Gill glanced up apologetically. "Sorry, I've given my number out to so many people I can't keep up with them. Seems like I'm the president of the lonely hearts club," he smirked.

Feeling like a klutz Lily, forged ahead. "So what do you want me to call you?"

"You can call me anything you like, but just call me, night or day," he said, his eyebrows hiking up and down.

Heat crept up Lily's neck, and she fanned herself. She didn't know if she should run or slap him. Hearing her number called, she stood on shaky legs and got her coffee and muffin. She couldn't help but feel his eyes groping her six. It was with mixed emotions she found her way back to the table.

"So, what are you studying?" His question caught her off guard and she took a sip of the hot brew and waited for her pulse to slow.

Knowing what Troy thought about her career choice, she was reluctant to answer. Bracing herself for what she knew would be an overreaction; she offered him a shaky smile.

"Criminal Justice."

The lines on Gill's forehead creased. "Oh, pretty heavy stuff for a …" his voice trailed off.

"For a what? A girl? So you don't think women should play with the *big boys*?" she taunted.

Palms held in surrender. "No, it's not like that. I just thought you'd say you were into fashion design or marketing, something like that."

Lily waved aside the comment. "My dad owns a

fancy security firm," she fibbed, "it seems interesting, and so I thought I'd give it a try. If it doesn't work out, I could always go to work for Wal-Mart as a rent-a-cop," her tone playful. "Anyway, the university has a great self-defense class, so don't try anything," giving him a nudge to the ribs. "And you? What's your major?"

Gill broke his muffin in half and shoved it into his mouth. After washing it down with a gulp of coffee, he dabbed his mouth with a napkin and cleared his throat. "When I grow up, I want to be an architect. You know, build giant edifices extolling the virtues of mankind."

Eyes wide, Lily glanced over the rim of her mug. "You don't look like the architect type. I had you pegged for a jock on an athletic scholarship."

"Sports? Nah, I'm not into sports, not unless you call Rugby a sport."

"Rugby? Isn't that 'a game for rich young boys to play,'" quoting from Les Miserable.

"Well, I was brought up in private Catholic schools all my life."

"So are you, some kind of rich kid?"

Gill shifted uncomfortably, and his color darkened. "I think I've said too much," remembering his uncle's warning. "I'd better be going."

"Wait," Lily protested, "you haven't finished wolfing down the other half of your muffin."

He relaxed back down and let out a tight breath. "My uncle said to stay away from you."

Nearly spilling her coffee, Lily's mouth gaped, her eyes flashing surprise. "Me? Why did he say that? He doesn't even know me."

Gill's expression went from cocky to apologetic. "I, I mean, he said to say away from girls like you."

A male student sitting at the next table glanced over. "Man in hole, stop digging."

Suddenly, the room burst into laughter as both Gill and Lily stared in disbelief. Had the entire room heard their conversation? Lily wondered. She felt the urge to crawl under the table. In a huff, she stood and marched from the coffee shop, leaving Gill with his mouth hanging open.

Chapter Thirteen

alking stiff-legged, Lily marched down the tree-lined sidewalk.

If it were possible, you could see steam ascending from her ears. Her mind replayed the warning Gill's uncle gave him. Stay away from her. Why? She wondered. Did he know her? How could he? She'd never met the man and yet for some reason, he didn't like her. A brush of movement caught her eye, and she whirled around. Was she being followed? Shivers ran down her spine and she wanted to bolt. Her dorm room had been ransacked, her character besmirched and now someone was following her.

Reaching for her can of mace, she resumed a steady gait and prayed she would have the courage to use it. Passing a row of windows, she glanced behind her. Her instincts were correct. She was being followed, but by whom?

She released a long-held breath and glanced over her shoulder. He was tall and wore a ball cap tugged over a mop of curly brown hair. The light-weight jacket covered a bulge leaving little doubt what was there.

With his face obscured from her sight, Lily was unable to get a good description of him, but one thing stood out . . . he walked with a limp. She made a mental note of it and scampered up the steps of Tahoe Hall, where her dorm room awaited her.

After making sure the lock was secure, she found her cell phone and punched in her dad's number. "Trace, I think someone's following me."

"I'd halfway expected it. Things are spinning out of control faster than a blown engine. Maybe you should come home until we get this mess sorted out." He didn't sound very convincing. Their condo had been broken into, so really, there was nowhere safe.

"Now Trace, you know I'm not one to run from a fight. Anyway, there's someone I've met," stretching the truth. There was something about Gill, which intrigued her and she couldn't put her finger on it.

"Lily, what about Troy, he's a nice guy."

"Trace," she guffawed, "you sound like an old goat herder trying to pawn his niece off to the butcher's son."

His phone beeped. It was an incoming call. "Look, Honey, I've got to take this. Think about what I said, be careful and don't be caught alone. Understand?"

Sighing into the phone, she said, "Yes, Trace. I've got my mace. Now take the call and you be careful."

The call ended and she walked across her suite. Peeking around the curtain, she scanned the street.

He was there.

Even from as far away as she was, she could faintly make out the tune he was humming. Something by Bach or was it, Beethoven. A cold chill ran the length of her back. The shadowy figure moved directly across from her dorm. The air in her throat turned to ice, and she yanked the curtain shut. Panting, she raced to the door and double checked the deadbolt.

***

It had taken Lily nearly a week to get comfortable walking the campus.

Even then, she stayed in a group. With her constantly looking over her shoulder, she was getting a cramp in her neck. Calling the campus police was always an option. But since her secret admirer never came closer than a half a block; never appeared threatening, she decided to watch and wait. She wondered if the man ever slept.

***

Wanting a cup of coffee and something to munch, she decided to take a chance and go to the library.

However, the idea of having Gill walk next to her would be a good excuse to call him. It could possibly ward off her unwanted shadow. A quick search of the school's registry provided her with the information she needed.

She dialed the number on the printout and waited. After several rings, it went to voicemail. "Yo dude, this is Gill. I'm either studying, *not,* or I'm talking with someone else. So try again later. You'll eventually get me."

Lily let a frustrated breath escape her lungs and hung up without leaving a message. *I wonder where he could be at this hour?*

Chapter Fourteen

The news of Rosa Tampico's murder hit Guillermo extremely hard.

She had been his nanny until his tenth birthday. She was the closest thing to a real mother he'd ever known. Now she was dead. Killed the same night as Father O'Leary.

Was there a connection?

He remembered his uncle telling Antonio Beretta about the jewelry box. Now she was dead. Whoever killed Rosa came to Father O'Leary's study seeking and finding it.

Now the two people most dear to him were dead, and it had something with that jewelry box.

To tell his uncle what he knew could prove disastrous. He knew how his uncle worked. Yet, he couldn't let these murders go unanswered. He had to find the guy who did this and make him pay.

The tattoo.

He had a tattoo on his left hand. Using the college data system, he did a search for gangs and tattoos. He found the tattoo belonged to a gang operating in the Sacramento Valley. They were primarily made up of illegals and were a violent bunch.

Not the type of people he associated with.

He picked up a pencil and began to sketch the face of the man who'd nearly killed him. At first, the going was slow, but as he added details, the face became more familiar. By the time he'd finished, he had a good likeness. Now he just needed to compare that with the state and federal face-recognition profiles.

He needed to talk to Lily. With her taking Criminal-Justice classes, maybe she could get into the university's database. If they could hack into the state's system, he could identify the killer.

"Lily?" She sounded pleased to hear from him.

"Am I interrupting something … this is Gill."

"No, I'm glad you called back."

"You called me?

"Yeah, thirty minutes ago. I didn't leave a message."

"What's up?"

He could hear her shift the phone from one ear to the other.

"Oh, it's nothing."

"C'mon, Lily. Don't blow me off. I'm really sorry about what my uncle said. I shouldn't have brought it up. Now, why'd ya call?"

A thoughtful pause.

"Okay," she sounded relieved to finally tell someone. "I'll give you the Readers-Digest version. A year or so ago, some guy tried to take advantage of me. He tried it twice."

"No way."

"Yes, way. He's some kind of doctor and the last time he tried it, he actually saved my life by taking out my ruptured appendix. So it's pretty weird. Anyway, short version, I think I'm being followed. Umm, I was hoping you could walk me to the library."

Gill's eyebrows shot up. "The library … funny you should ask. I happen to need to do some research there myself. I'll meet you outside your dorm in … let's say two minutes."

"Your dorm is further away than that. Are you going to fly?"

Jangling the keys to his Jeep in the background, he said, "Yee, in my trusty Renegade. See ya in two."

***

The dorm across the street from Lily's room provided the perfect observation post.

Unfortunately, it was too good. The body of the student who'd taken pictures of Lily through her window ceased quivering thirty minutes ago and was rolled up in a carpet waiting to be deposited in a construction dumpster.

No one was allowed to take pictures of Lily. Not without his permission and he wasn't giving it. Only one picture remained from that fateful night six years ago, and he was determined to get it back. Had his plans not been thwarted, he would have gotten it months ago. Now he had to watch and wait.

When her light suddenly went out, he sat up straight. It was too early for bed. Her roommate was still out, so he knew there was no other reason for her to turn the lights out unless it was to leave.

He hadn't bugged her room, yet. An oversight he planned to correct … soon.

Maybe tonight.

Standing, he prepared to follow her. If she was going for a walk or run, he would stay close. If she was meeting that brawny young man again, he might have to move up his plans. The thought of another man stealing her affection made his blood boil.

Headlights strafed his windows and he jacked backward. Once the vehicle parked, a young, physically fit college student jumped out and sprang up to the co-ed dorm where Lily appeared. The streetlight showed what he needed to know.

It was Gill.

It was time to initiate plan B.

But first, find out where they're going. If they went for a run, he would tag along. If to the library, that would complicate things.

They turned in the direction of the library.

He cursed.

Not having creds to get into the college library, he was shut out. He would have to wait and maybe catch a snippet of their conversation on the way back to the young man's Jeep.

A Jeep. He made a note to put a tracking device on it, tonight.

***

"So, what are you researching?" Lily asked as she logged on to the college's computer.

Guillermo sidled up next to her and watched. Keeping his voice at a library level, he whispered, "I need to access the state facial recognition database." He slid the pencil drawing in her direction.

Nose wrinkling, she asked, "Who's this?"

Not wanting to say too much, he chose to lie. "He's a guy who dinged my Jeep, and I wanted to track him down."

The lie seemed to satisfy Lily, and she scanned in the mockup. Fingers flying over the keyboard, she entered her name and password.

"My prof gave us limited access to that information, so I could count this as practice doing background checks. This is right up my alley."

He nodded, crossed his fingers and watched as a bank of faces sprang up on the screen.

"Bingo, well, not exactly bingo. That is just this month's cons. Let me broaden the search and bring in a side-by-side."

Guillermo kept his eyes on Lily as she went to work. She was really good at this.

Fifteen minutes of scanning faces and eliminating the obvious ones, females, Caucasians, Blacks, and older men, they found three matches.

Leaning close, Gull caught the light scent of Jasmine and vanilla. He inhaled deeply, and let it out. "You smell good. What is it?"

Lily was concentrating so much on the key identification points, she missed his question.

"I'm sorry, did you say something?"

He sagged back into his seat. "Nah, but that's the guy. I see a definite resemblance. Does he have an address?"

Lily clicked on the one he'd indicated and a complete

list of his arrest record, jail time, aliases, and addresses scrolled up. The problem, there were too many for one person to check out. And if someone came snooping at the wrong address, chances were, he'd be shot.

Or his query would bolt. Either way, he'd used up his good will. It was Lily's turn to start her research.

"What do I owe you?" he asked, hoping to lengthen the evening with another cup of coffee.

After checking her watch, Lily said, "It's getting late. Let's call it quits. I can always do this research some other time. It's not like it's an assignment."

Guillermo's face twisted into a question. "What were you going to research before I came along?"

Lily picked up her backpack, slung it over her shoulder. A few strands of honey shaded hair fell across her face. She swiped them aside. "Boring stuff like, a place called Santa Vern and a twenty-one-year-old kidnaping."

It was all Guillermo could do to keep from jolting upright. His palms grew suddenly sweaty, and he had to gulp his breath.

"What is it? Did I say something wrong?"

He waved her off. "Ah, nothing. I'll tell you about it sometime. How 'bout we get a cup of java; my treat."

It was what she'd hoped for all along.

"Yeah, that sounds great," glad it was his idea. Logging off, they exited the library.

A shadow moved parallel with them … listening.

Chapter Fifteen

With the media clambering for a quick answer, Giorgio thought it best to keep his head down.

No more break-ins.

No more killings.

No more bodies.

By the close of the week, the police were no closer to finding the murdered than they were when they started. And that was the way Giorgio liked it. He had purposefully waited, hoping the trail would cool off before he made his next move.

Earlier that evening, he'd called Antonio and arranged for a late-night exchange.

The jewelry box in exchange for a hundred big ones.

Leaning his scrawny shoulder against the door frame of Antonio Beretta's office, he waited for Carnes to leave.

Once he'd closed the door behind him, Giorgio shifted the toothpick he'd been gnawing on from the left side of his mouth to the right, just for variety. With a long glance at the closed door, he sauntered across the plush carpet and slouched into one of Antonio's cushioned wing-backed chairs. Propping a booted foot on the corner of his boss's desk, he asked, "How long's that old guy been with you, anyway?"

Antonio ignored the comment. "Get your boot off my desk."

With a shrug, he complied.

"You got the goods?" Antonio asked, his tone icy.

"Yeah, sure, boss. It's all here." As he spoke, he pulled the jewelry box from his backpack and laid it on the desk.

"Have you opened it?"

Looking offended, he said, "No, boss. I couldn't get my hands on the key. But with the proper motivation, I think I could." He wriggled his eyebrows. "You got the money?"

Reaching into his desk, Antonio moved aside his pearl-handled Colt 45, he grabbed a manila envelope. With a shove, he slid it across the polished desk.

A crooked smile exaggerated the long scar along his cheekbone. Greedily, Giorgio caught the envelope before it slid off the desk and broke the seal. In the wicked silence, he thumbed through the stack of money. "Not too bad for a couple nights of work. Word on the street is, O'Reilly's on the case. That spells trouble. You want me to take the guy out?" Giorgio asked, rubbing his hands like a kid in a candy shop.

Antonio spat out a curse. "You read my mind. O'Reilly's gotten too close once before. Take him out, but make it look like an accident. No witnesses, no loose ends. Now get out of here."

Antonio had neither the intestinal fortitude nor the backbone to kill someone himself. That's why he hired it out. He was a shadow of his father, but he had to keep up appearances. The crime syndicate Luciano built was showing signs of wear, and it was his job to keep it together.

Control.

It was all about control.

And he was losing it.

Maybe it was time to take things to the next level.

Ushering Giorgio to the back door, Antonio gave him a slight shove and sent him on his way.

"I'll be in touch."

***

The listening device Jimmy placed inside Antonio's office picked up every word.

The NVG's, or night-vision goggles, equipped with telescopic lens, gave him the ability to see in the dark from a safe distance. From his vantage point, he watched under a waning moon.

The fact that he wasn't able to stop Giorgio from killing Rosa, and the priest weighed heavily on his mind. He would have to make it up to him later. For now, his focus had to be on Antonio and Sanchez. But having overheard Antonio tell Giorgio to kill Trace, he knew he had to do something. If he broke his silence, it would jeopardize his neatly arranged disappearance. He could use one of his snitches, but that was risky. In the end, he hit 67 to block caller ID and sent an anonymous text to Troy Ashcroft's phone.

***

Shades of muted light filtered through the window panes forming a cross stitch pattern on the hardwood floor.

In the corner of the parlor, the aging grandfather clock faithfully transformed seconds into minutes and minutes into hours. At this late hour, Jimmy knew the kitchen staff, and housekeepers had gone home for the night. Only Carnes remained, and he had retired to his quarters.

Antonio had the place to himself. It wasn't unusual for him to be alone. Of that, Jimmy was certain. As a bachelor of forty-five, he had plenty of opportunities for a late-night liaison, but he'd passed on most of the prospects. For one reason or another, they did not meet his approval. They were either after his money or wanted to control him.

Control.

It was always about control.

It was going on midnight, and Jimmy was getting concerned. If his instincts were correct, Governor Sanchez would come tonight. He had to get his hands on that box before the governor showed up or all his efforts would have been in vain.

The jewelry box Giorgio left hours ago remained under Antonio's watchful eyes.

All he needed was two minutes to get in and out.

Two lousy minutes.

His chance came when Antonio left his office.

This was it.

This was the chance he'd been waiting for.

***

No sooner had Antonio disappeared, then Jimmy sprang into action.

With gloved hands, he picked the lock and eased the door open. Silently, he entered the office and pulled the door closed. As Antonio's steps receded, he knew he had only a few minutes to accomplish his mission. Crossing the hardwood floor, his foot found a loose board. It squeaked shattering the silence.

He froze, not breathing.

Seconds ticked.

Sweat beaded on his forehead, but he resisted the urge to wipe it aside. He couldn't leave any evidence of his presence.

After a few beats, he took several quick steps across the room. Blending into a dark corner, he checked the hall.

It was empty.

Good.

Silent as death, he turned his attention to the jewelry box. With a steady hand, he slipped the lock picking tool into the grooved hole and twisted. To his surprise, the action of the tumblers was smooth.

The lid popped open.

A smile stretched across his face.

The manila envelope was the evidence he'd sought across the years. It was one of the reasons he'd faked his death.

Now he had it.

Time to leave.

With care, he removed the envelope, replaced it with an old newspaper and closed the lid.

Voices down the hall.

He stuffed the envelope inside his jacket, and ducked into a dark corner.

Chapter Sixteen

Over the last fifty years of serving the Beretta family, Carnes had seen a lot.

And he knew a lot more.

Having made the decision to leave Antonio's employment, he began the sad task of packing his belongs. Over the years, he'd accumulated many gifts, mementos, and a host of memories. It was those memories he cherished most.

Swallowing the lump in his throat, he carefully wrapped each picture and placed them in a box. As he returned from making a trip to his car, the floor above him creaked. He was so familiar with every square inch of the mansion he could walk through it with his eyes closed.

Hearing movement in Antonio's office, his pulse quickened. He knew Antonio left his office. He also knew he was expecting a guest, but he was running behind. So who was in his office? Had Antonio returned to finish his drink? Had he missed his responsibility? Even though he intended on terminating his employment with the Beretta family, habits were hard to break.

Stepping into the lounge, he was met with a flurry of angry words. "What are you doing?" Antonio demanded.

"Just cleaning up, sir."

His answer didn't pacify his employer. He continued, "Will you be needing anything else?"

"No! You've been eavesdropping. That's what you're doing, old man. If it wasn't for my father, I'd have buried you in concrete a long time ago."

Carnes squared his shoulder. He had always treated his masters with respect and dignity, but this was the end, no more. "Sir, I've watched you and your father corrupt this city, and stood by doing nothing." His voice grew raspy.

"And what are you going to do, old man, kill me, say it was self-defense, and run to the police? I doubt it," he sneered. "I've got men at every level of government from dog catcher to Washington DC. I'm untouchable."

For a moment, Carnes wavered.

He had been loyal … too loyal.

The secrets he knew were enough to bring down scores of shell corporations. But if he spoke out, who would believe him? It would be his word against a bevy of lawyers.

"Okay, you win," he said, his shoulders slumped. "You've got my word and my silence. I'll be leaving your employment effective immediately. I needn't remind you of my years of service to your father, Luciano."

Antonio stepped from the doorway, and gave him a slight bow. "That's the only thing keeping you alive. But do not set foot in Sacramento again, or I may not be so forgiving."

Silently, Carnes nodded and stepped into the hall. He hated himself for being such a push-over. Why had he not stood up to the man? Why hadn't he found a weapon?

Maybe it wasn't too late.

***

Amber headlights traced a narrow swath of light, along the tree-lined road, in long, angular shafts.

Greedy shadows reached out with phantom fingers, grabbing and clawing at the limousine in a futile attempt to capture it. Yet the sleek vehicle moved with deliberation to its destination … the Beretta mansion.

It was all about control.

Finally, it came to a gentle halt in front of the sprawling building. It couldn't be called a home, that would imply a husband and a wife and a family.

Antonio was no husband.

Sanchez barely regarded him as a man. He was more like a leech, a bloodsucker.

From where he sat, the mansion was but a shadow of its glory days under the Luciano era. In his hay day, he entertained celebrities from rock stars to rock-ribbed conservatives to wobbly-kneed liberals and everyone in between.

The word *entertained* stuck in his psyche like a chicken bone. Were it not for Monica *entertaining* him, Luciano might not have ever gotten his hooks into him. But alas, women were his weakness … especially Monica.

Thinking back, he was amazed that his wife overlooked his proclivities. As long as he kept her in furs, booze and on the corporate board of every major contributor, she was satisfied.

Not happy … just satisfied.

It was all about control.

The one thing she lacked was a child. If the rumors were true, he had no difficulty in producing offspring with other women, yet when it came to his wife, he'd been an abysmal failure.

Then came the night of the accident.

The one which sent Monica O'Reilly to the hospital. He knew Anna overheard the one-sided phone call from the hospital. She knew it was serious. She had to have known if it involved Monica, it involved her husband and that meant it involved her.

Unbeknown to him, Anna followed him to the hospital. It was only later, he learned when she arrived, she found an inebriated doctor, an out of control medical staff, and her husband hovering over Monica and two newborn children.

Monica's children.

Possibly her husband's children.

She snapped.

Something inside her gave way to the dark side. In an act of desperation, she snatched the child wrapped in a blue blanket from his incubator.

As she made her escape, she noticed something. The woman Monica collided with was eight months pregnant. The child she was carrying didn't survive.

Seizing the opportunity, she quickly exchanged the names on the birth and death certificates. Then she placed the deceased child in the incubator where she'd taken the living infant. In the confusion, no one noticed.

Fifteen minutes later, she was gone.

***

Like Moses' parents, Anna kept her secret from her husband.

The only other person who knew her secret was Rosa Tampico, Anna's closest confidant. Fearing her husband's temper and unstable condition, she had two necklaces made each barring half a key. One with the letter L and the other with the letter W and a jewelry box where she placed Willie's birth certificate.

It was her insurance.

Then she placed it into Rosa's care.

As news of the child's abduction spread, Anna's name came to the surface. Rafael Sanchez's political aspirations hung by a thread.

Anna became a liability.

Under questionable circumstances, Anna took her life. The medical examiner listed her death as a suicide, and the media helped to perpetuate the lie.

***

Ten years later, Rosa decided it was time to move on.

The name Luciano Beretta was commonly spoken in the Sanchez household, and she quickly found a place on his staff. For the next eleven years, she served the Beretta family until Giorgio ended her life.

The soft rumble of thunder brought Rafael from his musings.

"Perfect," the governor muttered, "just what I needed."

His driver moved clumsily around to the door and opened an oversized umbrella. Without looking up, he grabbed the handle and splashed up the flagstone walk. With care, he reached the front door without getting too wet. Like a dog shaking off his coat, he shook the moisture from his outer garment and stored the umbrella in a container designed for that purpose.

Chapter Seventeen

Antonio had just taken his seat when the doorbell chimed.

Frustrated he had to do it himself, he made his way to the front door and swung it open.

"Good evening, Governor," he said ruefully. "I don't know where Carnes is. He usually does this sort of thing."

The governor grunted out an indistinguishable response. He didn't like being at Antonio's beck and call, but it was better than having him come to his office. He eyed his host suspiciously, then stepped into the foyer. After pulling off his coat, he hung it on the brass knob next to a dozen other brass knobs. Drips of rainwater fell to the mat and formed a puddle. "Have you got the necklace and jewelry box?"

Antonio cut his eyes in the direction of Carnes' suite. "Now, now Governor, let's not get ahead of ourselves. You asked me to do a job, and I did it. Let's relax a minute, get a drink and discuss how you're going to pay for it."

Sanchez breathed a curse. He wished he'd taken his Aripiprazole, an oral drug used to control antipsychotic tendencies. He never knew when he might have an episode, as he called them. They were coming more frequently since his nomination. He just hoped nothing happened tonight.

"My, my, my, Governor, you call yourself a Catholic? You may need to go to confession. Oh, that's right, I nearly forgot. Your friend, Father O'Leary, died tragically. What a shame." He shook his head sardonically.

Sanchez ground his teeth. "Look you weasel. You didn't have to kill him, did you? Couldn't your guy just do a simple bump and run?"

"No. The priest was responsible for closing several of my brothels. Cost me thousands," he huffed. "Now, let's drink to our success," he said, as he led the governor to the lounge.

The bottle of bourbon sat where Antonio left it. He grabbed another shot glass, poured two drinks and handed one to his guest.

"To our mutually beneficial business arrangement," he said, holding his glass out.

Sanchez muttered his agreement, tapped his glass and downed it in one swig. He waited for the burning sensation to stop and refilled the glass. As the alcohol spread to his extremities, his head cleared.

Antonio eyed him before downing his. "Now, there's the matter of being paid. How do you want to do it, cash or credit?"

The governor finished his second drink, poured himself another and followed Antonio to his office.

"Do you know someone ID'd your guy?"

Antonio released a mirthless chuckle. "I've got that covered. Like I told you, no one will connect me with the crime, especially not O'Reilly."

Sanchez steadied himself on the desk, then slouched into one of the posh chairs. Tipping his shot glass, he peered over the rim. "I don't care as long as I get what's inside that jewelry box."

Antonio downed another shot of Bourbon. "Well, let's get to it. That storm isn't letting up. You got the money?"

Sanchez reached inside his coat pocket, and Antonio froze.

"Relax, I'm just getting this," Sanchez said, pulling out a thick envelope. He shoved it across Antonio's desk.

Antonio loosened his grip on the drawer where he kept his Colt 45. It was his fathers and had seen more action than he cared to think about.

Eyeing the jewelry box, Antonio continued, "My guy wasn't able to get the key. How are you at picking locks?"

Ignoring his statement, Sanchez grabbed the box and yanked on the handle. To his surprise, the lid popped open with ease. "Is this some kind of joke?" his voice grew tense.

Antonio glanced down. A yellowed newspaper lay in the bottom of the box. Thrusting his hand inside, he sought vainly for the missing document. "I, I don't know what happened. No one has been in here or touch it. I swear."

The front door slammed, and both men reached for their guns. "It must have been Carnes. After him!" Antonio shouted, and dashed from his office.

"Oh no, you don't! You're not getting away that fast." The floor shook as Sanchez's boots pounded down the hall.

Things were spinning out of control.

Jagged streaks of white-hot lightning ripped the fabric of the clouds open. Sheets of rain began to spill from the tattered clouds. Deep, ponderous peels of thunder rattled the windows and the lights throughout the mansion went out.

Panic gripped Sanchez's chest as he felt his way along the blackened hallway. "Antonio, get back here you pig, or I'll kill you."

He was loosing control.

A shadow moved, and he pounced on him. The two men tumbled into the great room, knocking over a plant stand and bumping into end tables.

The room shook with the force of gunfire.

Glass shattered.

Wood splintered.

Chapter Eighteen

Hearing the commotion, Carnes, ascended the stairs and stopped as two men rolled across the floor.

Lightning flashed, and Antonio appeared on top of the governor, his hands pressed deeply into his throat.

Darkness enclosed the scene again.

Air swooshed with the movement of a heavy object.

It struck.

Someone groaned … fell.

Another flash of lightning revealed a gruesome sight.

Antonio, his head crushed, lay motionless.

Dark crimson drips slid down the walls, staining the curtains, spreading across the floor.

Carnes' heart slammed against his ribs like a caged animal clawing to get out.

Was his boss dead?

Who attacked him?

Where had his attacker come from?

He couldn't tell. Blood was everywhere. Another thunder clap split the night sky, illuminating the gory scene. As he waited for his eyes to adjust, footsteps coming toward him brought Carnes to full alert.

Was it in front of him or behind? He couldn't tell. Someone brushed past him. The shadowed figure grabbed the governor by the arms and began to drag him toward the front door.

Lightning flashed partially illuminating the hunkering figure. He was wearing a black coat … a black hat shaded his face.

Not knowing what to do, he waited, hoping the man wouldn't return. The grandfather clock sprang to life sending a jolt of adrenaline through Carnes' bony limbs. After twelve long gongs, it fell silent except for the ticking of seconds.

The passing of time.

The passing of a life.

The end of an era.

Finally, he bent over and checked Antonio for a pulse. It was as he suspected, his boss was dead … very dead.

***

Sanchez awoke with a jolt. He'd been lying in the grass for longer than he could calculate.

Above him, the angry sky wept heavy drops of icy rain, soaking his clothes, chilling him to the bone.

His mind still muddled.

What happened? Where am I? How did I get here?

Stabbing pain radiated from his head as streaks of red and yellow splashed before his eyes. Reaching up, he touched the source.

"Ouch," he winched pulling his hand back. Lightning flashed, and he glanced at his fingers. They were covered with blood. Looking down, his shirt was also covered in blood. Feeling for a wound and finding none, he forced himself up on shaky legs.

What's going on?

Swiping rain from his eyes, he tried to remember where he was. Another burst of lightning flashed revealing the ominous silhouette of the Beretta mansion. It loomed over him like a black hole waiting to swallow him. Like a zombie, he staggered forward until he reached the partially opened front door. He stopped, braced himself on the frame. Then stepped inside.

"Antonio?" His voice sounded hollow, vacant, foreign.

"Carnes? Anybody?"

Nothing.

Leaving a puddle of muddy, bloody water in the foyer, he felt his way back down the hall until he reached Antonio's office. His trembling fingers found the envelope and closed around it. He snatched it up and stuffed inside his coat. Ignoring the inert jewelry box which was the source of his troubles, he stumbled back out. As he forced his legs to carry him to the front door, another burst of lightning revealed the chilling truth. Antonio's body lay in a pool of blood ... his skull smashed, his shocked eyes stared blankly into nothingness.

Whose blood soaked his shirt, his or Antonio's?

It was all a blur.

The gun he'd brought with him lay across the room. He picked it up and shoved it into his pocket. He tried to make sense of what had happened. Had he blacked out? Had his condition gotten worse? All he could think of was Antonio's lifeless eyes staring past him.

The voices in his head grew louder, the images more vivid.

On unsteady legs, he plunged back into the storm hoping to reach his vehicle before passing out.

"Drive," he said to his driver, who stared as if in a trance.

"But—"

"Drive, get us out of here."

"Where to?"

"To the ranch," he cursed. "Use the service entrance."

It was only after he'd reached the mountain road that he realized he hadn't taken a breath. Gasping for air, he tried to force his frozen mind to thaw.

What have I done?

***

As Carnes wobbled to his feet, the front door burst open.

Heavy breathing turned his blood to ice crystals. Governor Sanchez staggered back into the house. His shirt was torn and bloody. His eyes, wild with fear, shock, and surprise, stared through him as if he wasn't there.

Fearing for his life, he backed into a shadowed niche and waited. To his surprise, the governor ignored the bloody corpse on the floor and wobbled down the hall, hands against the hall to support himself.

Not knowing what else to do, Carnes followed Sanchez down the hall and watched him stumble into Antonio's office. Shakily, the governor snatched the envelope from the desk and blindly bulled past Carnes, nearly knocking into him in the process. A moment later, he was gone.

After a long minute, Carnes realized he'd stopped breathing. Forcing his lungs to work, he grabbed the door frame for support.

What happened?

Had the governor murdered Antonio?

Who was that dark figure who dragged him outside and why had Sanchez returned?

Deeply shaken, he crept down the hall, slammed the front door shut and locked it. Then he returned to the bloody corpse.

What should he do? He couldn't just leave his boss there. Should he run? Leave the premises? Or should he clean up the mess?

That's what butlers do … clean up other people's messes.

Yes, he would clean up the mess.

Then leave.

Forever.

Using a handkerchief, he picked up the bloody poker and returned it to the fireplace. Then, with care, he repositioned the body to make it appear Antonio had struck his head on the hearth. It wasn't perfect, but he hadn't the time or the criminal mind to think of everything. He checked to see if the phone still worked.

It did.

He dialed 9-1-1 and covered the mouthpiece with a handkerchief. "There's been a murder at the Beretta Estate. Come quickly."

He ended the call.

Knowing he had about forty-five minutes before the police arrived, he quickly wiped the shot glasses and finished packing. After loading his car, he pulled the door to his suite closed.

Still shaken by the evening's events, he released a heavy sigh. With one last look at the mansion, which had been his home for over fifty years, he climbed into his car and started the engine. He wished his parting would have been on a happier note, but alas. Never in his wildest dreams could he have imagined this. A bitter tear formed and slid down a deep wrinkle on his cheek. He wiped it aside with a curse. Putting the car in gear, he cut his wheels and drove away.

Chapter Nineteen

When my phone rang at one-fifteen a.m., I knew something was wrong.

"Trace, are you awake?"

"I am now."

"What's up?"

"Trace, about an hour ago we got an anonymous tip. The caller said there'd been a murder at the Beretta mansion."

"A murder? Who was it this time?" I asked, the memory of my ex-wife lying at the bottom of the stairs still fresh on my mind.

Not missing a beat, Troy said, "It's Antonio Beretta."

My breath turned to ice. "How do you know he was murdered?"

"Because I'm standing over his body. His head's been smashed in. In my experience, that qualifies as a murder."

"Any idea who called?"

"No. How soon can you get here?"

I checked the clock. "I'll be there in twenty minutes, depending on traffic."

With Lily refusing to leave her college routine, I was glad I wasn't leaving her alone. Besides, she was focused on her studies, her self-defense classes and some guy named Gill, and not in that particular order.

By now, Wag was at my side. Ever the protector, he

was always ready for a new adventure. However, this didn't seem like an adventure, it was more like a black hole I was about to step into.

***

It took me nearly forty-five minutes to make the drive to the Beretta mansion.

Luckily, at that hour, traffic was light. The cup of coffee I snagged from a twenty-four-hour restaurant reminded me of the last time I changed my oil, only worse.

Patting the dashboard of my vintage Renault, I eased from behind the steering wheel and crossed the parking lot. Already, my powers of observation were on high alert. It was as much a gift as a curse. I saw everything, sometimes too much.

A light breeze stirred the rain sodden air. It was fresh with night blooming jasmine which climbed the exterior of the mansion. In the distance, a coyote yipped, an owl hooted and a frog croaked the night away. The crime tape, which defined the yard and front entrance, flapped lazily in the breeze.

Ignoring the officers working the lawn, I leaned under the tape and approached the front door.

"It's open." Troy knelt on the carpeted runner inspecting a muddy shoe print.

I pulled my cell from its case and began snapping pictures of the scene. It had been a long time since I'd seen such carnage.

"I see you've taken a page out of my book."

Standing up, Troy gave a practiced glance around the room. "I had a good teacher."

Chapter Twenty

The sleek limo pulled around to the back of the governor's sprawling estate and came to a gentle stop.

The governor, still shaken, got out of his car and staggered into his residence. *How am I going to explain a black eye and a knot on my head?* Unable to recall how he'd gotten blood on his shirt, he pulled it off, filled a utility basin with cold water and began to rinse it. Then he carefully doctored the knot on his head. *Had he really killed Antonio Beretta? And who dragged him into the yard?*

It was all a blur.

He'd lost control.

Fortunately, most of his staff had left for the night. And with the second Mrs. Sanchez away on a fundraiser tour for her favorite charity, he had little to explain.

After taking a couple of aspirins, he showered and got ready for bed. But sleep came in snatches as faces, voices, and images invaded his dreams.

***

Pounding on his bedroom door ended Sanchez's fitful sleep.

He cursed the morning and crawled from his bed. With a quick jerk, he pulled his silk robe from its hanger and tugged it on. Jamming his feet into a pair of slippers, he padded to the source of irritation.

Giving the door a quick yank, he swung it open.

"Yes?" he growled.

His chief of staff straightened. "Sir, I'm sorry to have to wake you, but you have visitors."

"Visitors, I didn't think I had anyone scheduled until eleven o'clock." His sharp tone set his chief of staff on his heels.

"It's the police. They say they have a few questions, and were quite insistent."

The Governor huffed. "Call my attorney, get him here ASAP, and stall them until he arrives."

"I thought you would say that. I've already put in a call to him. He should be here within the hour."

"Good, take the police to my study, and let them wait until I get there."

With a glancing look over his shoulder, his chief of staff lowered his voice. "Sir, what is this all about?"

Sanchez mopped his brow, "I'm not sure, Carl. I'm guessing it's got something to do with Father O'Leary's murder. He was my spiritual leader. Maybe they're following up on a lead. I just hope I can help them. It seems so senseless, killing a man of the cloth." His voice grew thick.

***

Thirty minutes later, Sanchez let out an irritated huff as

he entered his office. Taking a seat behind his impressive desk, he eyed the detectives warily.

With John Dutton, the latest in a string of attorneys, sitting to his left, he waited for Troy to begin.

"Sorry to get you up at this hour, sir, but with the press and chief demanding answers, well—"

Sanchez waved aside Troy's poor attempt at warming the icy atmosphere.

"Just get on with it, detective," he growled.

Nodding, Troy pressed ahead. "Yes, sir. With your attorney's permission, we'd like to ask you a few questions—"

"If it's about Father O'Leary's death, let me say for the record, I think it is despicable. A real tragedy. The man was a saint, a real saint."

Troy pulled his pen from his pocket, double clicked it, and made a note on his notepad. "Thank you, Governor. Were you two close?"

Nodding, Sanchez hoped he'd led the conversation away from anything related to last night's events. "Oh yes. He was my spiritual leader. I confided in him on many occasions."

Leaning his elbows on his knees, Troy narrowed his eyes. "Yes, we knew that. In your conversations, did he ever say he thought his life was in danger?"

"No."

"Did he have any enemies?"

The governor shifted uncomfortably. "None that I can think of. Like I said, the man was a saint. Everyone loved him. He was not only a man of the cloth, but a community leader. He was responsible for closing several local brothels."

Troy sat up straighter. "Yes. We knew that too. So don't you think that created a few enemies? Did he ever mention to you that he had a somewhat tenuous relationship with Antonio Beretta?"

Sanchez felt his mouth turn to sand. Eyeing his attorney, he waited.

"Uh, that would be confidential between my client and his priest, and since Father O'Leary isn't with us any longer, your question is moot."

Troy inhaled, and let it out slowly. Checking his notes, he continued. "Sir, could you tell me your whereabouts last evening?"

The governor glanced at Mr. Dutton. "Again detective, is this really necessary? My client is a busy man. His itinerary is an open book. Check with his secretary, she will tell you he was at a private dinner with a few of his strongest supporters. They will confirm his whereabouts."

Sanchez began to breathe again. *This guy is good. I wonder what I'm paying him ... probably not enough.*

Crossing his leg over his ankle, Troy continued, "Then you won't have any trouble explaining how your thumbprint got on a shot glass we recovered from Mr. Beretta's residence, would you?" It was a bluff. There were no fingerprints in the shot glasses. The one they found on the edge of Antonio's desk could only prove he'd been there. He needed to prove the governor was there that night. He fixed his steely gray eyes on Sanchez and waited.

Sanchez's tongue stuck to the roof of his mouth like a

leech. "Oh, that. I stopped by earlier to see my old friend. We had a few drinks, and I left," he blurted before Mr. Dutton could stop him.

"About what time was that?"

His attorney jumped to her feet. "Detective, really, is this necessary? My client's a busy man."

"Quit the theatrics, Dutton. You're not in a courtroom … yet."

Turning to face the governor, Troy waited.

A trickle of sweat popped on the man's forehead and rolled down his temple. "I don't know, somewhere around three."

Troy made a note of it. "Now, I'm a bit confused, were you in his office or the lounge?" Troy knew the answer but hoped to catch the governor in a lie.

Narrowing his eyes, Sanchez tried to recall which room he had been in. To say the wrong room meant he was hiding something. He needed a way out. Taking a quick glance at his lawyer, he held his breath, praying he would bail him out.

"Look, Detective you're on a fishing expedition, and we both know it. I'm sure you have better things to do than quibble over where a guy drinks his booze. I've been to the Beretta estate. He has liquor stashed all over the place. The guy is a lush."

"Was a lush," Troy shot back, not missing a beat. "And by the way, how did you get that black eye, governor?"

"What do you mean, was?" the attorney asked.

"I mean *was* because someone killed Antonio last night. Now, Governor Sanchez, I asked you a question.

Did you have your drink in his office or the lounge?"

Sanchez stood, and jabbed his finger in the air. "You filthy scumbag. You're just trying to trick me. I'll have your badge for this." His voice thundered. "I needn't remind you, you work for me. How dare you come into *my* home and accuse *me* of murder."

Jumping between the governor and Troy, attorney Dutton interrupted his boss. "I'm sorry fellas. This conversation is over. If you want to ask my client any more questions, you'll need a warrant. I won't sit by and have you grilling him, not in his own home. Now, if you'll excuse us, we have a plane to catch."

Troy took a deep breath and glanced at me. I knew he'd been outmaneuvered. Standing, I motioned toward the door.

"Yes, well, how about we continue this down town, say … tomorrow about this time? Oh, and be sure to use the back entrance. We wouldn't want the press to get a hold of this, now would we?" Troy's voice carried a threatening tone.

As he eased the door closed, he paused a moment and listened.

"And just where did you get that shiner?"

I tugged him out before Sanchez threw us out.

Chapter Twenty-One

It had been a long, sleepless night.

My mind wrestled with who and why someone would kill Antonio Beretta. Yes, he had his enemies, but none came to mind. To actually bump him off would be paramount to all-out war between the crime syndicates.

Once again, Troy's phone call interrupted the little sleep I'd had since going to bed.

"Hey buddy." Troy's tone was annoyingly chipper.

I peered angrily at the clock. Troy was quickly becoming persona non grade. "Whaddya want?" I growled.

"Can we meet for coffee? I got some things I want to run by you."

It was six-thirty.

"Don't you sleep?"

He chuckled.

I huffed.

"Yeah, I got in a few winks."

I gave Wag an indolent look and slid out of bed. "I'll meet you at our usual coffee joint in about an hour."

"Make it forty-five."

Call ended.

Grumbling, I padded to the shower.

Exactly forty-five minutes later, I arrived a bit harried.

Troy arrived after me.

He took a seat across from me, placed his order. While we waited, he laid a small listening device on the table.

"Where'd you find that?"

Troy fingered it a moment. "In Antonio's office under his phone."

I felt my pulse quicken. "Got any idea who's been eavesdropping?"

"No, but it's the same kind we use in the department."

I mulled that over a second. "What else?"

Troy took a sip of coffee and added more sugar.

"That will clog your arteries and make you fat."

He smiled at my observation. "We got a tip Antonio put out a contract on you."

I nearly spilled my coffee. "A contract? I'm honored."

"Apparently, he doesn't like what you're working on."

"You mean what we're working on. Remember, you got me into this mess."

Palms up, Troy shook his head. "You're right, but I'm getting paid. You're a volunteer."

"More like a conscript, if you ask me."

"Touché my friend, touché. I'd lay odds whoever is doing the eavesdropping sent me that tip." Taking out his notepad, he flipped a few pages. "We found two gunshot holes in the wood paneling. I got a couple of guys running ballistic tests on the bullets. As to Antonio, he died from blunt-force trauma. But the blood splatters were on the other side of the room." He paused to check his measurements, a trick he'd learned from me. "His body was twenty feet from the blood splatters, and it was positioned to make it look like he'd stumbled and struck his head on the hearth. The problem is, his wounds were on the back and middle of his skull, not the front."

"Meaning?"

"Meaning he was struck from behind."

"And the murder weapon?"

"I'll get to that. It appears Antonio put up quite a struggle. He had hair and skin under his nails, plus he had someone else's blood on his shirt. There are muddy footprints in the foyer, down the hall and all around the house."

All of this I already knew, but I was humoring my friend. "Hmm, what do you deduce from that, Sherlock?"

Troy shrugged. "We have three sets of shoe prints and only two people, not counting Carnes. I am guessing Sanchez came in after the rain started. Actually, it looks like he came in twice. We also have a third person coming in and leaving."

I'd noticed the umbrella, but didn't say anything, hoping Troy would.

He did.

I was glad.

"We're working on the prints on the umbrella, but as wet as it was, I'm doubtful we'll get any."

I could have guessed that. Our meal arrived, and we waited until the server finished before continuing.

"Okay, what else?" I asked, in between bites.

Troy pulled a sheet of clear paper from his pocket and handed me a pencil. "Can you draw the floor plan of the downstairs?"

"I can do better than that. I took several pictures. They're in my phone." Fishing it from its pouch, I brought them up."

"Send them to me. I'll have my team go over them."

"How about fingerprints? We're you able to lift any?"

"As you know, there were two shot glasses in Antonio's office, but they'd been wiped clean. Apparently, the killer was pretty thorough."

"How much alcohol was in Antonio's blood?"

Troy paused to think. "Quite a bit."

"Any fingerprints on the bottle?"

Troy's expression darkened. Lifting his cell, he hit speed dial.

"Who are you calling?"

The lines on his forehead wrinkled. Lifting a finger, he said, "Al, get someone to check for prints on the bottle of Bourbon."

He waited.

"You have? Any matches?"

His face flattened.

The call ended, and he blew out a breath.

I felt my blood pressure spike.

"Yeah, we got one. It belongs to Governor Sanchez."

My stomach knotted. "Are you going to take him in?"

Troy shifted uncomfortably. "That's not my call. I'm heading to the judge to get a bench warrant. You want to join me?"

"I thought you'd never ask. What else?"

Troy rechecked his notes. "I'm guessing it was the Butler, in the dining room with the candlestick."

The wrinkles around his eyes deepened. Something I'd noticed recently in Troy's face. His-fresh-out-of-college face showed signs of wear. In a few years, he'll look as haggard as me. I didn't wish that on anyone.

"We went to question Carnes, but his apartment had been cleaned out. We've got a BOLO out for him, but so far, no luck. As to the murder weapon, it had to have been something mighty heavy to have done so much damage. I mean, the guy's skull was—" he paused at the thought of the gruesome sight. "I'm guessing Antonio and Sanchez got into an argument. The two men fought. Carnes grabbed the fire poker, swings and accidentally kills his boss. In a panic, he wipes off the blood, places it back where he found it and leaves. I think we have an open-and-shut case of manslaughter at best."

Sitting back, I rubbed my chin. "Sounds plausible, but why were they fighting? And how about the extra muddy shoe prints? Whose were they?"

A long pause.

Finally, I broke the silence. "My guess is someone else whacked Antonio, and then, for some unknown reason, dragged Sanchez outside. Then he returned and repositioned Antonio to make it look like an accident."

"That sounds really crazy."

"What about the guy with the clean shoes? Did he kill Antonio before or after the muddy-shoe guy came and went?"

The divot between Troy's eyes deepened. "I just don't know."

***

Troy's cell phone sprang to life interrupting his thoughts.

"Hello?" It was Lily.

I used this opportunity to make a pit stop. When I returned, Troy was still on the phone. I hated eavesdropping, but I had little choice since we had not finished our meal.

By his tone, I could tell he was disappointed. My guess was, it was a butt call. Troy's shoulders sagged, and he gave me a wounded look.

"Hey, while I got you, could we hook up sometime? It's been forever."

An uncomfortable pause.

Troy shifted the phone to his other ear. "A coffee shop on campus? Sounds great." He sounded nonplussed. "I'll be there as soon as I get off." He shot me a glance.

The cell phone went silent, and he pushed the off button. Not that it was necessary since Lily had already bailed. She was probably on to her next phone call … the one she really wanted to make.

"I didn't even have a chance to ask her where the coffee shop is."

I felt Troy's pain.

"Women."

"Yeah … women."

Silence.

Time to refocus. We had a killer to catch.

Chapter Twenty-Two

The following day, Troy laid out his argument for the judge to issue a bench warrant for Governor Sanchez.

He granted it with one condition, to keep it out of the press. By then, I had a splitting headache. I hoped the drive into the country would relieve it.

It didn't.

When we arrived at the Beretta mansion, the pain in my head had grown exponentially. I popped four Advil into my mouth and dry-swallowed them.

Troy pulled up in front of the stately mansion and got out. The yellow tape sagged with moisture and small caution flags, defining the ragged shape of a body, waved lazily in the breeze. I noticed the panked down grass the previous night, and I wondered if anyone else would.

Someone did … probably Troy.

Good man.

"Follow me," he said, calling my attention forward.

We padded down the stairs to Carnes' suite. A uniformed officer stood guard at the door.

I thought that odd but said nothing.

As we approached, he stepped aside and pushed the door open. We stepped across the threshold and surveyed the space. Two things struck me. One, Carnes was well taken care of and two, he was a meticulous resident. The suite boasted the latest offset lighting and recently purchased couch and chairs.

Lily would have approved.

So did I.

Troy brushed past me and circled the area. A brief inspection revealed what I had already guessed.

Carnes was gone.

His belongings, his pictures, his collection of classical music CDs. Gone.

"Looks like we've got our prime suspect," Troy said. He pulled his pen from his pocket protector and double clicked it.

"Hold on a minute, Troy. Antonio died from blunt force trauma. I don't think Carnes had the strength. He is what, eighty something?"

Troy nodded. "Ya got a point. But it doesn't take that much force to crack a man's skull, especially with an iron poker."

Glancing around, he continued, "This looks like he packed up everything he could get in his car and ran."

I inspected his medicine cabinet, his pantry and utility closet. Nothing unusual. "Well, it was no secret, he and Antonio didn't get along."

Troy rubbed his chin and scanned the room. The carpets had been vacuumed, the dishes put away, even the towels were folded. "You might have a point. First, he packs then he whacks."

Turning to the uniformed officer, Troy asked, "Any luck at finding Mr. Carnes ..." He looked at me with a quizzical expression. "Is Carnes his first name or last?"

I jammed my hand into my pocket. "You got me. All I've ever known him as Carnes."

Troy returned his gaze to the officer. "Give me your notepad." He jotted down a quick description of the man and handed it back. "I want him brought in for questioning. Oh, and see if you can run a background check on Mr. Carnes, credit cards, checking account, bank account. The usual stuff."

By now, my headache released its grip on my head. Returning to Antonio's office, we continued looking for anything the other guys had missed. "You know Trace, before I got the call that he was murdered, I was going to come up here."

Glancing up, I cocked an eyebrow. Oh? Why's that?"

"We checked the church's security system. Can you believe it? Churches needing security systems and weapon detectors. What's this world coming to? Anyway, they had a camera pointed at the door leading into the sanctuary. We got a good, clear picture of the creep as he entered the sanctuary. The guy's name is Giorgio Romero Vincent. He has a rap sheet a mile long, and he's one of Antonio's goons."

"Why would Beretta want a priest killed?" I wondered.

"Not just killed, robbed."

"Robbed? Robbed of what?"

"That's what I was going to ask Mr. Beretta."

I straightened and began a studied look around the room. "Has it occurred to you, whoever killed Rosa Tampico also killed the priest then came here to rob and kill Antonio? Maybe he was the victim of a bigger plot?"

Troy's eyebrows knit. "How do you figure that?"

Pulling the wadded newspaper from the bottom of the jewelry box, I flattened it out.

Troy's eyes widened. "CHILD SNATCHED FROM SACRAMENTO PRENATAL UNIT."

"Look at the date."

While Troy read the article, I dug in my coat pocket. "Take a look at this?" I handed him the folded newspaper clipping Jimmy had given me.

The muscles in Troy's jaw tightened. The date, April 4th, 1992 though aged and worn by time was clearly visible. "Who gave you this?"

"Jimmy."

"Why?"

"That's the date Lily was born, the same date my son was abducted."

"What?"

"I'll tell you about it on the way back."

***

"What do you mean you and Troy have a bench warrant for Governor Sanchez?"

My call to Cami wasn't going too well. Despite the poor quality of the connection, her frustration came through crystal clear.

She continued, "You should have asked me. I could have told you where he was the other night."

"True, but we have a good set of fingerprints, which put him in Antonio's home the night of the murder."

"No, you have a good set of fingerprints, which

proves he visited there sometime but not that time."

The woman had a point. He could have come and gone before the murder took place.

"You could clear up a lot of questions if you corroborate his story or deny its validity. He told us he'd visited Antonio earlier in the day, but left sometime around three. Is that true?"

For a moment, the phone fell silent. "You know. If it wasn't you asking, I'd be screaming for a lawyer?"

"Yeah, but it is me. It's better you tell me now rather than having Troy question you downtown." The thought of Troy and me playing Good Cop, Bad Cop brought a smile to my face.

Cami must have read my mind. "You two make a pretty good team with your Good Cop, Bad Cop routine. I bet you guys would get a real kick out of pulling that on me." She paused as if she were considering her options. "If I tell you, it's got to be completely off the record. Understand?"

I shot Troy a glance as he changed lanes and headed for the Governor's ranch. We had only a few minutes to get our facts lined up. "Cami, you know where this is leading. If he is in any way connected with Antonio's death, Troy will have to arrest him."

Seconds ticked.

"You still thinking?"

"I am, I am. Listen, the governor had a late-night meeting with Antonio. The only reason I know this is because he sent me and the rest of his staff home early. I overheard him calling his driver—"

"How about his driver? Maybe we should question

him first."

"Well, there's something funny about that. Usually, his driver is on call 24/7 but he's gone missing. I mean, for days. I tried to reach him but got his answer machine."

"So who drove the governor's car?"

"I don't know. He never drives himself, so he must have called on his backup driver."

"You have his regular driver's number? We can pay him a visit. If we find out he took Sanchez there earlier than the time of the murder, then your boss is off the hook."

"Look, you're playing with fire. You know that, don't you? Troy could be demoted to dog catcher, and you might end up on the bottom of the Sacramento River wearing concrete shoes."

That thought had occurred to me, but getting to the truth outweighed the consequences. And, if it meant getting my good reputation back, all the better. The question was, to what extent was I willing to go to do that? Whose life was I willing to put in danger? Lily's? Cami's? … mine? And what lines was I willing to cross in order to put a bad man away? Could I sacrifice my integrity to see justice prevail?

I didn't have the answer, at least not yet.

But I was working on it.

"Cami, the last thing Jimmy did before disappearing was to give me a scrap of newspaper dated April 4th, 1992."

"So, what's the big deal about that?"

"Cami, don't you remember? That was the date my

son disappeared."

Silence.

"How does that tie into Antonio's death?"

"It may not, but when I was in Antonio's office, I found an old newspaper stuffed in Lily's jewelry box."

A sharp intake.

"It was dated April 4th, 1992. The headline read; CHILD SNATCHED FROM SACRAMENTO PRENATAL UNIT. Now I'm not sure if that was originally in the jewelry box, but it's got to mean something, and Jimmy knew it. I think he was trying to warn me or give me a clue, something."

"Okay, I'll help you, but you've got to promise me you'll keep my name out of it. He's been acting really strange lately. And remember, I still have to work for him."

Sanchez's paranoia and mood swings were legendary. I let out a long-held breath. "I promise. Now what his driver's address?"

I jotted it down.

"How about we go out for a pizza and a movie this weekend?"

"What, and see, 'The Godfather'?"

"Very funny. Seriously, we need some face time."

Cami breathed heavily into the phone. "Yes, we do, but not this weekend. I'm heading out tomorrow to set up a ten-day campaign sweep throughout the mid-west. I'll return on Monday."

"All right then, Tuesday it is. I'll pick you up around five. That's unless I'm not swimming with the fishes."

"Not very funny, Trace, not very funny."

Chapter Twenty-Three

I t was obvious why the only empty parking slot in the apartment complex sat unoccupied.

Troy's lips turned down apologetically as the stench from the dumpster drifted our direction.

"Do you think you could have chosen a worse parking slot?" I asked, fighting back a wave of nausea.

"Hey, it's the only one around. Plus, it's out of sight." Holding his breath, he exited the vehicle, slammed the door and came around to my side. "Okay, here's how we're going to play this. We'll tell him we have evidence, which puts him inside the Beretta home around 11:30 p.m., and watch his reaction."

"Sounds like a plan. Let's roll."

The narrow hall leading to Larry Street's apartment reeked with body odor, trash, and booze. The grungy walls sported an assortment of folk art, graffiti and gang signs.

"Not my kind of place," Troy whispered as we neared apartment number 215. Pulling out his identification, he held it up in clear view of the peephole. With his other hand resting on the butt of his weapon, he nodded for me to knock.

After giving the door a crisp knock, the door inched open. I shot Troy a quick glance. "Shall we?"

He pulled his gun and held it pointed down. "You go high. I'll go low, on three."

I mimicked his action, my heart ticking up a notch.

"One, two, three!"

Troy kicked the door open and rushed in. "Police, hands up!" his tone commanding.

I swung my weapon in a smooth arch while Troy covered the right. Stepping further inside, he took a quick glance around the corner.

The throbbing of music from the apartment next door drowned out our movements as we searched the small apartment.

"Trace," Troy called from the bathroom. "Get in here quick."

I stepped next to him, holstered my weapon and let out a breath. "No need for these here."

"You got that right."

"He's been dead for a while by the condition of the body," I said, fighting back a wave of nausea. I'd seen death lots of times.

Never did get used to it.

I didn't know if that was a good thing or not.

Kneeling down, I inspected the body. "Looks like he'd overdosed or got a bad batch of hooch." The floor was littered with drug paraphernalia.

"It could be a setup made to make us think he OD-ed."

Troy holstered his weapon. "I'll call it in."

"You'd better hurry. You have a hot date with Lily in a little while."

"Oh shoot," twisting his wrist, he glanced at his

watch. "I totally forgot."

I smiled. "Don't worry, Lily runs on solar time. She's late for everything."

As we stepped back into the hall, an elderly woman wearing a soiled housecoat and puffing on a cigarette excused herself as she ambled past.

"Uh, ma'am?" Troy said.

She paused and cocked her head. "Yes?"

With his badge visable, he continued, "I'm Detective Troy Ashcroft, and this is my partner." He intentionally didn't state my name for obvious reasons.

"Could I ask a few questions?"

The woman took a long drag from her cigarette and surveyed us suspiciously. I could see the wheels turning and felt a pinch in my wallet.

She exhaled through her nose and nodded. "What's this all about? If it's about that hit and run, I've been meaning to get down to the police department and explain. You see, I'm diabetic and if I don't get my MEDs, well, I could go into—"

Troy waved her off. "No, ma'am, it's not about that hit-and-run—"

"Well, if it's about my good-for-nothin'-son, he can rot in—"

Frustrated, Troy raised an index finger to silence her ramblings. "No, ma'am. We just want to ask you a few questions about your neighbor."

She took another drag.

More smoke.

More ashes. Hand against the wall to support herself, she narrowed her eyes. "So whaddya want to know?"

Troy pulled his notepad out and double clicked his pen. "When was the last time you saw Mr. Street?"

Finger to her chin, she searched the ceiling as if the answer floated somewhere up there. "Oh, I'd say about two days ago."

"Did he have any visitors recently?"

Glancing down, she gave me an appraising scan. A coy smile brightened her face. "Mr. Detective, you didn't mention your partner's name. What can I call you?"

My heart ticked up a beat. I'd hoped by now my notoriety had faded. Her knowing my name could raise a lot of questions.

Fortunately, Troy came to my rescue. "Ma'am, you were about to tell us if your neighbor had any visitors."

Her eyes refocused on him. "Come to think of it, he did have a visitor. A big guy in a black leather coat, hoodie pulled down. He kinda looked familiar, but I wasn't wearing my glasses. I hate those things. They make me look ten years older." Pulling an ancient pair of pink horn-rimmed glasses from her housecoat; she fixed them on her nose. "There, now I can see you. Don't they make me look older?" she paused, her enlarged eyeballs switching between us.

I suppressed a chuckle.

Troy smiled. "Yes, ma'am. They sure do."

She gasped and yanked them off. "Why you—"

"—Thank you, ma'am. Have a nice day." Backing away, we beat a hasty retreat. Once in the car, Troy wriggled his eyebrows. "Looks like you have a taker if Cami doesn't work out."

"Very funny, Troy. Maybe if things don't work out

between you and Lily, she could hook up with the guy who's been following her."

The smile on Troy's face dissolved. "She hasn't said a word about a guy following her."

I extended my hand and patted his shoulder. "Well ol' buddy. I guess a girl is entitled to a few secret admirers. Maybe it's that big guy she met at church the other day."

Furrowing his brow, Troy shook his head. "Oh that guy. I think it's a passing thing. She's trying to make me jealous."

I couldn't hide my chagrin. "Looks like it's working."

Chapter Twenty-Four

With his attorney's help, Governor Sanchez was able to call in a number of political favors and avoid going downtown and be interviewed by Detective Troy Ashcroft.

That, however, didn't stop Dutton from grilling him first. "Now Governor, I need you to level with me, where did you get that shiner and don't tell me you slipped in the bathroom."

Sanchez sagged back into his chair. His morning was not turning out like he'd planned. "You're my attorney. Anything I say to you is under the attorney/client privacy act, right?"

Dutton heard that line of questioning before, and it usually meant his client was about to deliver some incriminating news. He bobbed his head reluctantly.

This is going to cost him big time.

Sanchez played with a pencil nervously. "I got this," pointing at his bruised cheek, "because Antonio attacked me. Yes, I was there the other evening. I went there to collect something of value he was holding for me. A big storm blew in and knocked out the power. Everything went black. Someone grabbed my belongings and ran. Antonio and I chased him, but we got tangled up. I thought he was the thief. He must have thought the same thing. Anyway, someone struck Antonio on the noggin and killed him. It could have been the thief, or the butler. I don't know. I must have passed out. The next thing I know, I'm outside in the rain."

Dutton sat still as a wooden Indian, listening.

Sanchez pressed on. "I don't know how long I laid there … long enough to get soaked. Once my head cleared, all I could think of was getting …" his voice trailed off.

"You were saying, Governor?"

Sanchez blinked. "Yes, as I was saying, all I could think of was get, to the car and leave."

That was the whitewashed truth.

The seasoned attorney remained motionless. His face bore neither compassion nor condemnation. The tension in the room was palpable. It was a tough spot for an attorney and client to be in.

"Self defense with no eyewitnesses is a difficult position to defend, especially for a presidential candidate. Not to mention your history with the deceased, who had ties to a crime syndicate. But first, you have to remember, you haven't been charged with anything … yet."

"Yet, that's the operative word. Isn't there something better you can come up with?" Sanchez's question broke the wire-tight atmosphere. "You and I both know it's just a matter of time before the media gets wind of this. My opponent will have a field day."

"Which is why we need to get ahead of this. I'll call in a few favors. First, we need to let the police chief know he has a couple of rogue investigators doing opposition research on a law-abiding, presidential candidate. We need to make you the victim of a smear campaign. Get the public behind you. Let's try this case in the public forum long before it ever goes to the courtroom. From what I understand, Trace O'Reilly is a consultant on this case. We can make this look like this is nothing more than his personal crusade against you."

The knotted lines on Sanchez's face loosened.

"It would help if you had a witness, someone who was there, who saw it all, who could corroborate your story."

Sanchez stared blankly at a distant point on the horizon. If only his driver could speak up.

Loyalty and Fidelity.

Loyalty.

Fidelity.

Dutton jotted down all the information Governor Sanchez gave him and released a tired sigh. "Okay, I've got enough to work on. My advice to you is, don't talk to the press, don't talk to the police, and especially, don't talk to O'Reilly and that nosy detective."

Chapter Twenty-Five

roy and I were just entering the precinct parking lot to fill out the report concerning Larry Street's murder when the dispatcher called.

"Sergeant Ashcroft, the chief wants to see you ASAP."

"I'm just pulling into the station."

"Any idea why the urgency?"

"Can't say for sure, but he just got off the phone with Sanchez's attorney. It wasn't a friendly call."

My stomach knotted.

The color drained from Troy's face.

"You want me to join you?" I asked as Troy cut the engine.

He gripped the wheel. "Do you think I should text Lily and tell her I'm running late?"

"Sounds like Lily is the least of your worries. Who knows, this may only last a few minutes. C'mon, I'll go with you. Maybe he wants to award you for your diligence."

"I doubt that."

***

Chief William Jenkins was in one of those rare moods.

The kind which spelled dismissal for anyone who crossed his path. We entered the precinct overflowing with detainees, crying children, angry spouses and frustrated and overworked police officers. One step inside the processing room and a heavy silence descended. Sympathetic eyes watched as if we were going to the gallows.

"You wanted to see us, chief?" Troy's question went unanswered for a long moment.

When the chief finished scrawling a handwritten note to his secretary, he handed it to her, and she scurried from the room.

The glass door clicked shut. "Sit."

We sat.

He stared at us.

We stared back.

Finally, he placed his elbows on his desk, clasped his two beefy hands together and peered at us like we were a couple of naughty school children.

"Troy, Troy, Troy, what are we going to do with you?" It wasn't the kind of question he was expected to answer.

We waited.

"I understand you and your *partner*," he spat out the word as if it left a bad taste in his mouth, "have been trying to dig up dirt against my friend, the governor."

"Sir, if I may say—"

The chief cut him off with an icy stare. "No, you may not. For now, you are off the case. I'm assigning you to desk duty until further notice. Have I made myself clear on that point?"

Troy nodded sullenly. Although I was not an employee, I was under no illusion that he would not throw my butt in jail if I stepped out of line. I also knew my chances of getting my old job back were quickly evaporating.

He continued, "I just got off the phone with Mr. Dutton, Governor Sanchez's attorney. It seems that you two knuckleheads are working for the opposition party. There's got to be a law against that. If there isn't, I'll have internal affairs find something we can use to keep you occupied until you learn not to meddle in the wrong people's business. Oh, and by the way, the guy we caught on camera, the one who bumped off the priest … got hit by a dump truck and died at the scene. I call that poetic justice. Now get out of my sight." His booming voice rattled the glass enclosure which was his office.

We reentered the processing area where officers pretended to work. I knew they were silently cheering the chief's decision.

So much for working here, I mused.

As the doors of the precinct closed behind us, I glanced over at Troy. He looked as stunned as I felt the day I was arrested.

"Well, think of it this way, now you can spend more time with Lily."

He hiked an eyebrow. "On my salary? Maybe I should use this time to hunt for a more lucrative profession."

I chuckled. "You could try a life of crime. I hear it pays better, and you'll get on the chief's good side."

***

Gill parked the dump truck back where he'd found it and got out.

It was his first attempt at driving something that large, and his legs trembled from working the pedals. Between the clutch, the brake, the gas pedal and all those gears, it was nearly too much to handle. The truck, belonging to one of his uncle's construction companies, hadn't been used in months and was an unwieldy beast.

He'd talked the crew chief into giving him truck driving lessons, but the man didn't show up. After waiting an hour, he decided to try driving it himself.

As it turned out, the truck was more than he could handle. He'd clipped several bumpers, ran two red lights and to top it off, hit a man running across the road. In his defense, the hooded man came from some grungy apartments and dashed directly in his path.

Since he didn't have a CDL or permission to be driving the truck, he panicked and kept going. Using a garden hose, he washed off the blood and hair from the bumper and left. It would be his little secret. Maybe next time, he'd have the crew chief show him how to downshift. Until then, he'd keep it to himself.

Chapter Twenty-Six

The afternoon dragged on as if it dreaded yielding to the night.

By the time Lily's last class ended at four-thirty, she and her classmates were ready to party. It was Friday, the end of a grueling week. It seemed the profs had conspired together and piled on hours of assignments.

To top it off, this was the start of basketball season, and the university had an all-night dance planned to take place in the stadium. It was all Lily could do to keep up. With her still taking experimental treatments, Lily's energy level had plummeted, yet, she pushed on.

Keeping a steady pace, Lily left the university library on her way to the dorm. As she brushed past an overgrown hibiscus bush, shiver-flesh crept over her. Something moved. She took a quick glance over her shoulder, but lost sight of whatever or whoever it was. A moment later, a gloved hand grabbed her. The other covered her mouth and dragged her into the shadows. Struggling to free herself, she bit into the glove.

"Ouch," a muffled voice uttered, but the grip didn't weaken.

Focus, Lily, focus. She tried to remember her self-defense lessons.

In a quick move, she grabbed the man's hand, and did a loop-de-loop, twisting his hand behind him. With adrenaline racing through her veins, she kicked the man's legs out from under him. He groaned and tumbled over. In a quick move, she jammed his face into the ground.

The man struggled to break her grip, but the more he fought, the higher she yanked his arm. With her knee jammed into the small of his back, she grabbed his hood and pulled it off.

"Mr. Carnes?"

He groaned his ascent.

"Why are you following me?" She weakened her hold on him.

"Miss Lily, if you'll release me, I'll tell you."

She unlaced her fingers from his, rolled him over, and helped him to his feet.

Coughing and rubbing his wrist, Carnes straightened and glanced around. "Lily, you are in grave danger." His voice was strained and low.

"Danger, what kind of danger?"

Palms down, he tried to suppress her anxious tone.

"Lily, you must listen to me. There is a man following you—"

"I know. I thought it was you."

Shaking his head, Carnes steadied his gaze. "No, I came to warn you. That man, Dr. Peterson. He's still out there."

Lily's pulse quickened. She knew instinctively her life was in danger.

"Also, you need to know that Mr. Beretta is dead."

"Dead?" Lily's eyes grew round as saucers "How do

you know?"

Keeping his voice low, he whispered, "Because I was there when it happened. Now listen, don't believe what the news says. They are accusing me of the murder, but you must believe me when I say, I am innocent. I didn't kill Mr. Beretta. Do you understand?"

Her lips trembling, Lily nodded. "Yes, I believe you. But what are you going to do?"

After taking a glance over his shoulder, Carnes swiped the sweat from his brow. "I don't know."

"Can't you go to the police?"

Fear registered on Carnes' weathered face. "The police cannot be trusted. This thing is bigger than you know."

"Why not go to Troy, you can trust him."

"Because he might shoot first and ask questions later."

Taking him by the arms, Lily steadied the shaken man. "No, he's not like that. You can trust him."

The white-haired man straightened and locked eyes with Lily. "Honey, there's something else you must know."

Lily braced herself.

"Lily, I am your grandfather on your mother's side."

Hand to her throat, Lily gaped at him. "You're my what?"

His lower lip trembled, and a tear coursed down his cheek. "You're grandfather. Let me explain," his throat closed with emotion. He dragged his hand across his eyes. "Your mother and I had little in common. She was ashamed of me, and I disapproved of her immoral lifestyle. We seldom spoke and when we did, it usually ended badly."

"But why haven't you told me this sooner?"

Carnes' lips trembled. "Heaven knows I wanted to, but the time was never the right. I wanted to explain a few things and give you these." He sucked in a shaky breath. Reaching inside his coat pocket, he withdrew a bundle of envelopes. "I had planned to give these to you the night Sanchez's birthday, but Monica told me, in no uncertain terms, to stay away from both of you."

It was all Lily could do to keep from reaching out and hugging the elderly man. Finally, she gave in. Arms extended, she pulled him into a long embrace.

"I don't even know what to call you."

He pulled back and took her by the arms. "Call me Granddaddy."

She did.

"And now you must warn your father. There's no time to lose. There are some very important documents which someone is willing to kill for. Rose Tampico and Father O'Leary were only the first. There may be more." He turned to leave. "I'm afraid I'm getting too old for this sort of thing."

"Wait? Where can we find you?" Lily asked, biting back tears.

"Tell him to call this number." He thrust the bundle of envelopes and a crinkled business card with a cell number on it into her hands. By the time Lily read the number and looked up, he was gone.

Chapter Twenty-Seven

Sanchez sneered as the door closed behind Dutton. Retaking his seat, he suddenly felt lightheaded. It had been a while since he'd taken his medication, and he was having trouble concentrating. Voices began to ring in his ears, and he felt himself drifting. No, this isn't happening, he told himself but try as he might, he just couldn't seem to grasp reality. Struggling to breathe, he loosened his tie and swiped at his face. Fingers trembling, he dug into his pocket for a pill bottle. He worked the lid off, popped two pills into his mouth and forced them down.

Breathe.

Wait.

Breathe.

He had to stay in control.

As his mind cleared, he realized he was in no condition to meet with a wealthy donor, let alone entertain guests. He dialed his secretary. "Millie, cancel all my appointments, I'm not feeling very well."

"I'm sorry, Governor. Is there anything I can do for you, call your wife or the doctor?"

"No, that won't be necessary. Tell my staff to take the rest of the night off. Oh, and have the kitchen send up a light supper, maybe then I'll feel better."

"Yes, sir, right away."

Sanchez replaced the phone to its cradle. Numbly, he began sifting through a stack of papers that had beckoned his attention for weeks. Ignoring the sandwich and chips which the cook brought in an hour ago, he tried to get Antonio and that night off his mind.

It wasn't working.

After another hour, his neck ached and his bladder demanded relief. Any other time, he would have spent the day on the golf course or did an interview.

Anything but this.

He was losing control.

By the time the sun had dipped over the horizon, he was exhausted. All he wanted was to go to bed early. Maybe tomorrow would be a better day.

As he prepared to shut down his computer, an instant message sprang onto the screen.

"You've got mail," a female voice intoned.

He tapped in his email address and began scanning through the list of messages. The most recent one popped up. It read, 'I saw what you did.'

His breath turned to ice.

He reread the message. *Who was this and what did he mean?* His mind scrambled for answers.

Pushing himself up on wobbly legs, he made for the door. An instant before his trembling fingers turned the knob, his private cell phone rang. Fumbling, he reached into his pocket and pulled it out. After pressing the green button, he forced out a husky, "Hello?"

"Are you alone?"

The voice was unfamiliar ... muffled.

"Yes, who is this?"

"Who I am isn't important. What I have is. We need to meet … alone."

"Why, so you can kill me? No way. I'll wait until my security detail arrives. You won't get within fifty yards of me."

A low chuckle percolated through the connection. "See that red dot?"

Sanchez's eyes swept the room. They stopped on the mantle.

"That red dot indicates exactly where a bullet will go if I squeeze the trigger. And right now it is trained on your head. So again, we need to meet. I have a business proposal to offer you."

Feeling lightheaded, he clutched the door frame. "Okay, but it's got to be discreet. I don't want the press to get wind of this. You understand?"

"Of course, no cameras, no press, no witnesses." His last word sent a chill down the governor's back.

"Where and when do you want to meet?"

The caller shuffled some papers, and he guessed he was conferring with a map.

Sanchez scribbled the location as the caller rattled it off. It was an abandoned warehouse on the outskirts of town.

The call ended, and he stuffed the folded the paper into his pocket.

He was losing control.

Twisting his wrist, he checked his watch. Eleven-thirty. No time to assemble his security detail, no time to set up a trap. He was going to have to face this guy alone.

He hated being alone.

It is the reason he'd sought the company of Monica O'Reilly.

It was the reason he'd sought the company of others.

It was all about control.

Chapter Twenty-Eight

L ily's encounter with Carnes left her heart pounding.

Forcing her legs under her, she dashed up the stairs and stumbled into her dorm. It took ten minutes for her breathing to normalize and her mind to clear. She grabbed her cell phone and punched the preset button, letting her father know she had an emergency. The moment she did, the screen flashed and the phone died.

"Great," she muttered.

She'd been so tired the previous night, she'd failed to put her phone in the charger, now she was paying for it. She dug through her handbag and found the battery charger and attached the two, but it would be several minutes before her phone could be powered up. While she waited, she began grabbing a few of her belongings and tossing them into her overnight bag.

"Hey girl, what on earth are you doing?"

Lily jumped. Sucking in a sharp breath, she blurted, "Mikala, you scared me."

Mikala grinned. "So, you are going off with your boyfriend?"

Lily's cheeks pinked. The idea of letting a guy touch her immorally repulsed her. She'd seen her mother in action. Seen her use her womanly wiles to tempt men, get them to yield. They were putty in her hands. It was her idea for Lily to dress provocatively that night when she was a tender sixteen and flaunt herself at Sanchez's birthday party. It was part of her 'training,' as her mother called it. If she followed her mother's example, she would probably be dead … like her mother.

Mikala's question snapped her out of her thoughts. "No, my dad isn't feeling very well, and I'm going home to check on him."

Standing in the doorway, Mikala crossed her arms and huffed. "What, and miss the all night dance? No way are you going to bail and miss a good hazing that easily." Mikala, a member of her sorority, showed no sign of letting her escape.

"Yes, way. I'm the only one who can take care of him," she fibbed, but it was the first thing that popped into her head.

Hands on her hips, Mikala shouldered the door frame. "You gotta be kidding. I just saw you and your dad talking, and he looked fit to me. A bit hunched over, but healthy enough. So you can forget blowing out of here."

Lily slumped to her bed. She knew she wasn't going to get out of it that easily. And lying more would only complicate matters.

"Okay, but you gotta promise me you'll stick with me everywhere I go. Someone is following me."

Mikala dropped in next to her and looped her arm over Lily's shoulder. "Girl, I'd be surprised if you *didn't* have someone following you. Anyway, it's probably that guy with the chiseled ABS, tight gluts and piercing blue eyes."

"I, I don't know about that."

Eyeing Lily incredulously, Mikala crossed her arms. "He just so happens to be the hottest dude on campus. He's even hit on me a couple of times."

"Yeah, to hear him talk, he's got every girl on the campus's cell phone number. But he sure is cute." The dreamy expression on Lily's face only lasted a moment.

"Well, if it's any consolation, I'll be on you like white on rice."

Mikala's assurance didn't do much to relieve her fears, but at least she knew she wouldn't be left alone. Maybe her would-be-attacker wouldn't be at the dance. Maybe she could give her roommate the slip and get off campus when things got going.

She hoped the latter.

***

Arm in arm Mikala guided Lily into the football stadium where hundreds of undulating bodies swayed and bobbed.

With the volume of the music nearing jet engine levels, it made talking impossible. Even thinking a cogent thought was limited. The youthful energy was impulse driven. The air was pungent with cigarette and marijuana smoke. With as much alcohol as was being consumed, it was a wonder anyone could stay on their feet.

As the evening's festivities dragged on, Lily realized Mikala had gotten distracted. A quick check, she realized time had slipped away from her. It was going on eleven-thirty, and she needed to get going. Taking a deep breath, she slid behind a tree. After waiting a few beats, she dashed in the direction of her car. Thankfully, she'd had the foresight to stash her backpack in the shrubs near the parking lot.

***

It isn't easy being a six-foot tall white male.

That's what Nelson Peterson thought as he tried to make himself inconspicuous in a crowd of partying college students. If he got too close, Lily's roommate would spot him, and that would screw up his plan to nab her. However, if he strayed too far, she might slip through his fingers again, and that he couldn't allow. He'd waited so long to consummate their wedding. If it weren't for her bungling father, he would have done so years ago. And then there was the matter of her emergency appendectomy. He couldn't sit by and let her suffer and possibly die. He loved her. And one day she would come to understand that, but for now. He had his needs and waiting was not an option.

Chapter Twenty-Nine

❝Where am I going to get that much money?" The governor muttered under his breath.

Just because he was a governor didn't mean he walked around with a bucket of money. However, there was the money he brought to Antonio's office. It was unmarked and unaccounted for. He'd made sure of that. Though soaked from rain, the envelope was still intact. It would have to do. His next obstacle was to shake his security detail? He'd done it once, he could do it again.

His breathing tightened, and his palms grew sweaty. *I'm getting quite good at leading a double life.* He congratulated himself

Reaching into the desk drawer, he found an extra weapon in addition to the one he'd taken to the Beretta's home. It served him well as a businessman. It would serve him well tonight. Get back what belongs to him in the first place. Tie up a loose end and maybe he could get out of this conundrum unscathed. After checking the magazine, he chambered a round and slipped it into his coat pocket.

With a quick move, he flipped off the lights and left his office. A check in both directions told him the hall was clear. After waiting for the roving camera to pan in the other direction, he slipped into the hall and stealthfully made his way to the private parking deck.

To one side was a small booth where his driver hung out. There was an easy chair and a TV, and a refrigerator which he made sure was well stocked. He motioned to his driver who stood crisply and followed him.

"We're taking my personal car. I'll give you the directions after we get on the main road." The man nodded, not speaking, which was okay with the governor.

Once they were seated and belted in, the driver pulled his cap down further, glanced into the rearview mirror and backed up. With the service entrance unguarded at that hour of the night, the driver kept his headlights off and nosed the car along the tree-lined stretch of blacktop which skirted the property. It was only after they'd reached the main highway that he flicked them on and increased his speed.

Pulling the folded paper from his pocket, Sanchez said, "Take me to the corner of North Tenth Street and Vine. Park the car so it can't be seen and wait until I return."

The driver nodded. Fifteen minutes later, he slowed his speed and inched down the long stretch of decrepit buildings. Ahead, a set of headlights flashed. He returned the sign and pulled the car to a halt near a set of concrete steps.

"Wait here, and keep the engine running," the governor said as he dropped the extra gun on the front seat of the car. "Keep this handy in case someone tries to steal the car. I'm going to meet a man in that building. He said to come alone. If he sees anybody, he might get spooked and shoot me, so stay here. Understood?"

The driver nodded.

***

Sanchez fingered the revolver in his pocket.

After buttoning his coat, he stepped from the car and made his way across the open space. It felt like a rerun of an old western movie where the hero faced down the bad guy at high noon. Only he wasn't sure who the bad guy was. He had his skeletons in the closet, but so did the man he was going to meet.

Taking a cautious step, he moved further from the car. It was as if he was descending a path from which he would never return. But he was used to dark paths, his condition made sure of that. Columns of condensation followed him, and the chilled night air cut through his coat.

The man who called this meeting indicated they meet inside the warehouse, out of sight from unwanted eyes. Sanchez's lungs constricted, but he followed him into the aging building. Darkness closed in around him as the door slammed shut. A shiver ran down his back, but his feet held firm.

This was no time to run.

Once his eyes adjusted, he moved to the center of the building where a single shaft of dirty light illuminated a jagged square of concrete. Glancing around and seeing no one, he began to wonder if it was a trap.

"Breath," he told himself.

"Over here," the command came from somewhere outside.

Cautiously, he advanced deeper into the cavernous building until he reached an open bay door. His breath caught in his throat. A hooded man stood, a gun leveled directly at his chest.

With a quick flip of his wrist, he motioned Sanchez toward a set of concrete steps.

He obeyed.

Stepping into the amber glow of a single streetlight, Sanchez shuddered. "This place gives me the creeps," he muttered.

Despite the cold, large beads of sweat formed on his brow. Ignoring them, he wiped his slick hands on his coat and moved within ten feet of the man.

"I take it you have something of value, and you want to make an exchange," the governor's voice was hoarse, raspy.

The hooded man threw back his covering.

"Jimmy," Sanchez said, not hiding his surprise.

"Yes, Governor, it's me."

"It's been a long time. I heard you were dead. Where have you been hiding?"

"Doesn't matter. You wouldn't have found me."

"We found your wife."

"That you did, and you're going to pay for it."

"I figured. How much?" reaching into his coat.

Jimmy made as if he was going to shoot.

"Relax, I was just getting your money."

"Slowly."

It was all Sanchez could do to keep from dropping the envelope, but he managed.

"Show me the papers," Sanchez demanded.

In the dim illumination, he could see Jimmy move imperceptibly. "I ought to kill you and take these papers to the press. I'm sure they would have a field day with them. Bribery, extortion, government cover-up."

"It was the cost of doing business. How was I to know Santa Vern was a nuclear dump site? I had to recoup my losses. One day you'll thank me. Consider this your contribution to my success."

"And my wife? Can her death be considered part of your success?"

Palms up, he took a step back. "Now, Jimmy, that was none of my doing. I told Antonio to go easy on her, shake her up a bit."

"He killed her," Jimmy's voice cracked.

"I'm sorry. I truly am."

"That doesn't bring her back, does it?"

"No, no it doesn't. Antonio is dead if that's any consolation."

"It's not. But maybe a couple million will ease the pain. Now toss the envelope here."

Time was up. Sanchez stalled long enough.

Movement to his left caught Jimmy's attention.

Someone lunged for the gun.

In an instant, he was caught in a life and death struggle. The powerful man who'd emerged from the shadow twisted his gun-hand. He felt the bones in his wrist shatter, followed by excruciation pain. All at once, a gunshot shattered the night.

Jimmy staggered backward, clutching his chest. His legs buckled, and he toppled forward. Steaming blood pooled around his quivering body.

The next few moments became a blur.

The gunshot, the envelope, the information, the shooter … it all ran together like the blood staining the concrete.

The sight turned his stomach, and he retched. Wiping his mouth with the back of his hand, he steadied himself on the railing and dashed up the steps taking two at a time. His leather boots pounded heavily on the concrete floor as he raced across the cavernous building.

This wasn't how he'd planned it.

Not at all.

In the darkness, his head struck an iron beam. His legs went out from under him, and he landed hard on the concrete. Orange and red streaks flashed across his eyes.

Time slowed to a crawl. Unaware how long he'd been unconscious, he glanced at his watch.

Eleven-forty.

Had it only been ten minutes?

Scrambling to his feet, he peered around. He'd lost his weapon. It lay ten feet from where he'd fallen. His legs barely cooperated with his mind, but he willed them to work. He scooped it up shoved it into his pocket and lumbered to the exit.

Once outside, the night closed in around him. Hiding him. Embracing him.

Ahead, his car sat idling.

But his driver was nowhere to be seen.

Where could he be?

"Not good, not good," he muttered.

Fear did what common sense could not. He scrambled across the vacant parking lot and reached his vehicle.

No more shots.

No more dying.

Good.

Chest heaving, heart pounding, he reached his car and leaned heavily against it. Staring at his trembling fingers, he thought, *I doubt I could shoot someone now if I had to.*

Glancing up, he saw his driver. "Help me get in."

Without a word, his driver complied.

After he'd had taken his seat, he put the car in gear.

"Drive, get us out of here, now!"

A moment later, the car spun its wheels, fishtailed and left the grisly scene.

Chapter Thirty

Lily kept moving, her shoes kicking up small swirls of dirt with every frenzied step.

With any luck, she would be off campus before anyone noticed. Tightening her grip on her overnight bag, she took one final glance over her shoulder. Not seeing the figure materialize in her path, Lily slammed into a hulking figure with a bone-jarring crunch. Gasping, she found herself sprawled on the lawn.

A shadowy figure loomed over her.

"Gill?"

"Yeah, it's me," he said, tucking in his shirt.

"What are you doing out here?"

The corner of his mouth inched up into a half smile. "I could ask you that same question. It's the all-night dance. I was just getting back from a hazing. Boy did they rough me up," looking at his soiled shirt.

Lily narrowed her eyes. "Is that blood?" In the yellowed gloom of the streetlight, she couldn't be certain.

He unconsciously ran his hand over his chest and shifted his weight from one foot to the other. "Uh, yeah, like I said, the guys in my society sent me through the paddle line. I must have gotten a bloody nose." He touched it and gave her a pained expression.

Lily's heart skipped. She wanted him to enfold her in

his arms and tell her she was safe, that she had nothing to fear. But that was just it … she feared what she might do if he did.

He scuffed the ground in a boyish way. It was as if he wanted to say something.

"Where are you going anyway?"

Lily picked up her overnight bag and slung it over her shoulder. Peering up into his eyes was like looking into a deep well, one she could drink from for the rest of her life.

"Gill, I just got some disturbing news, and I need to see my dad. I'm really scared."

He stretched out his arms enfolded her. They were both warm and strong … and sweaty, but at that moment, she didn't mind. Burying her face in his chest, she drew in a deep breath. The aroma of his woody cologne invigorated her. She felt her resolve weaken.

"Babe, you're trembling. What's got you so spooked?"

"I'm being followed."

She felt his chest rumble as a rich, throaty chuckle bubbled up. "I'm not surprised. I've been trying to hook up with you all week."

She blinked.

Am I being paranoid? Wait, what did Carnes say? She refocused.

"Look, could you walk me to my car? I need to go."

"Now? The party's just getting started? Anyway, won't he be sacked out? Wait, isn't he that investigator whose—" Gill stopped mid-sentence.

Lily pulled away enough to catch the subtle change in

his demeanor. "Whose what?"

Gill dropped his arms, and jammed his hands into his pockets. "Babe, this is heavy. I heard on the news something about the police investigating the murder of that Catholic priest. Said the investigation stalled so they brought in a guy named O'Reilly. Isn't he your dad or step-dad?" His eyes probed hers.

She squirmed under his gaze. Her mind scrambled for answers.

Something didn't make sense.

The police didn't usually announce things like that. If they needed outside help, it was done under the radar.

Stepping back, Lily tried to think.

"Yeah! There's a lot of people with O'Reilly as their last name just like there's a lot of Sanchezs. For all I know you're the governor's kid. What are the chances of that?"

Gill's eyes widened. "Umm, look, it's late. I gotta bail. Big test tomorrow. If I don't get some head-time I'll fail the class."

His thinly veiled excuse didn't ring true. Saturday classes had been canceled. So why did he lie? Biting her lower lip, she caught a glimpse of her car. "That's okay. My car is just over there. I'll be a big brave girl, and get there without your help." Taking a steadying breath, she gripped the strap of her overnight bag and jogged toward her car. As she did so, she felt his eyes following her.

"How about we hook up later tomorrow?" His voice followed her all the way to her car.

"Text me," she said, not looking back.

Something wasn't right, but she couldn't put her

finger on it.

***

He'd been so close he could almost taste it.

Nelson shrank deeper into the shadows. This guy was becoming a problem, and he had only one way of dealing with problems.

As the taillights of Lily's car disappeared around the corner, he considered killing the young man but ruled it out.

Not here.

Not now, but soon.

Very soon.

Chapter Thirty-One

Troy's cell phone sprang to life puncturing his consciousness.

He reached for it, missed and tumbled out of bed. It slid across the floor. Unable to stand with his feet entangled in the sheets, he belly-crawled to where the buzzing device lay. By the time he reached it, it had gone to voice mail. He muttered a not so happy phrase, punched in the number, and waited. After following the prompts, he retrieved his messages.

"Troy, get your butt down here." It was the chief, and he didn't sound happy. Squinting at the clock, the digits eleven-thirty-five mocked him. "Doesn't anyone sleep?" he mumbled. "Might as well make two people unhappy." He dialed Trace's number.

"Trace, are you up?"

Giving the phone an ample yawn, Trace groaned. "I am now. What's with you? Don't you ever sleep?"

"Crime doesn't and neither do we?" Troy said, regretting it the moment it escaped his lips. "The chief just called me, said to get my tail down there. You want in?"

Trace cleared his throat. "I'm in. I'll be there in twenty minutes, depending on traffic." It was one of those meaningless sayings people say. This one was common among Californians.

***

Thirty minutes later, I met Troy outside the chief's office.

I handed him a cup of organic coffee, I perked before leaving. He took a sip, wrinkled his nose. "Don't you believe in sugar?"

"What? And ruin a good cup of Joe?"

Troy didn't smile. His set jaw and ridged stance told me he was just as unhappy to be called downtown as me. Scanning the room, all the old memories of long days and longer nights came back. On one hand, I missed the excitement of the hunt. On the other hand, I hated the politics.

"You have any idea why he called you?"

Shaking his head, Troy glanced around at the empty desks. I followed his gaze, glad the place was deserted.

"No, but we're about to find out."

Pushing into the chief's office, Troy entered with me trailing behind. We were met with two fiery eyes.

"You boys seen this?" the chief asked, tossing tomorrow's paper across the desk.

Troy caught it and gasped. GOVERNOR SANCHEZ IMPLICATED IN BERETTA MURDER.

Plopping into one of the overstuffed armchairs, Troy continued to read. "I don't get it. How could the press get this when all we did was ask him a few lousy questions? We didn't even bring him in for questioning."

Crossing his arms, the chief leaned forward and peered over his glasses. "We have a leak in the department. That's how."

His secretary buzzed in, cutting off his inevitable tirade. Troy breathed a frustrated sigh.

"Yes?!" The chief seethed.

The short one-sided conversation did nothing to lighten the chief's mood. He slammed the phone down and leered at us. "Okay, Troy, I know I put you on desk duty, but I'm stretched to the limit. I was just informed that there's been a shooting in the warehouse district. It's at the corner of North Tenth and Vine. I want you to get down there and check it out."

Jumping to his feet, Troy extended his hands. "But sir—"

The chief matched Troy's move. "Don't 'but sir' me. I'm still the chief around here, and I'm telling you to get yourself out there. Now!" he growled. After a beat, he took a deep breath and plopped back down in his chair. "Look guys, with the news spreading like wildfire about investigating the governor, I think it best to give it a rest. Heck, I'd bet good money it was the governor himself or his lawyer who tipped off the newspaper in the first place." By now, his face had returned to its normally flushed color, and his tone had softened … a bit.

Troy's shoulders sagged. It was not in his nature to give up on a hunt. Not when he smelled blood. Turning to me, he lowered his voice. "Look, Trace, if you want to go home, you're welcome to. You don't need to waste your time checking out a mugging."

I narrowed my eyes. "You woke me from a deep sleep, now you're telling me to go home? Forget it. Who knows, I might see something you overlooked."

Troy offered me a weak smile. "Fat chance of that, but you could try. Let's go. I know of a Krispy-Kreme donut shop with its red light on."

"Bring me some when you get back," the chief called after us.

"Forget it," we said in unison.

Chapter Thirty-Two

A fine mist sprang from the automatic sprinkler system just as Lily arrived at her condo.

"Great, now I've got to take the long way around to the front door," she muttered as she pulled into the parking deck.

She got out of her car and scanned the area looking for anything unusual. All the neighbor's cars were parked in their assigned spaces, but one was empty … her dad's. That bothered her. He was usually home at this hour. Maybe his clunker finally gave up the ghost. She had her, 'I told you so,' speech ready.

Mace canister in hand, she carefully made her way to the front door. She found her key and let herself in.

"Daddy?" her voice echoed throughout the house. *He's probably asleep.*

A dark shadow moved, and Wag nudged her with his nose. She jumped, releasing the canister. It clattered to the floor and rolled under a chair.

"Oh, Wag. You scared me to death." Her heart pounded so loud in her ears it nearly deafened her.

After turning off the alarm system, she knelt and looked him into his deep brown eyes. "I know. You want to go for a walk. You always want to go for a walk, but not now."

Wag's tail drooped, and he sauntered to his food bowl. Lily, still holding her breath, tiptoed down the hall to her dad's bedroom door. As she eased it open a crack, Wag brushed past her and jumped on the bed. In the dim light, she could see the bed was empty. Guilt gnawed at her conscience for thinking his car had broken down. He could be stranded anywhere. Now she was really worried.

Slumping on the corner of the bed, she cradled Wag in her lap and rubbed his neck. "No wonder you have to go. I bet daddy hadn't been home all evening … probably with Cami."

Hearing her name, Wag's ears perked up. "Yeah, that's right. She's a keeper." Standing, she padded into the living room. "What am I doing talking to a dog? I guess that's better than talking to a Rugby player." A dreamy smile tugged at the corners of her lips as she thought about Gill.

"Oh Gill, why do you have to be such a hunk. Everyone loves Gill. Big, handsome, charming, Gill. But there is something mysterious about you and I'm going to find out what it is."

Chapter Thirty-Three

It took five minutes for us to place our order and get a box of fresh, hot donuts.

I was in donut nirvana. The coffee failed to meet my high expectation, but I didn't complain since Troy was footing the bill.

With traffic virtually non-existent, we arrived in Sacramento's warehouse district in a matter of minutes. The area had seen better days. Many of the mill houses lining the streets were boarded up or battered in. Trash and uncut weeds accumulated along the chain-link fence protecting the rusting building.

"That looks familiar," Troy pointed out as our headlight swept across a beat-up pickup truck."

I cocked my head as we passed it. "It looks like Jimmy's. I got the tag. You want me to call it in?"

"Yeah, call it in while I check inside."

I did.

When I finished, Troy returned with an evidence bag. "Get a load of this," he said, handing the bag to me.

It was a map and lists of names.

The radio crackled. It was the dispatcher confirming the ownership of the pickup.

My jaw tightened. I feared Jimmy had gone rogue or worse.

"Trace."

I knew something was wrong the moment Troy called my name. Dreading what I might find, I left the evidence bag on the seat and followed Troy's flashlight beam.

Jimmy's body lay in a pool of dried blood. A ragged, ugly hole gaped where the bullet exited his back. There was no evidence of a robbery or a struggle. The reason for him being there, and the knowledge of who shot him, died with him.

I forced down the lump in my throat. "He was a good man. It shouldn't have ended this way. Do you think he had anything to do with any of these murders?"

Shaking his head, Troy took one last look at Jimmy's body. "It's hard to say, but my gut says yes. He said he was going to try to find who killed his wife. He may have, and it cost him dearly."

"He should have left things well enough alone," emotions clogged my throat.

Angrily, I picked up a loose brick and tossed it at the building. It struck the aging building and shattered the silence. "I wish I had tried harder to talk him out of it. I just stood by and said nothing." The tension in voice was palpable.

Stepping next to me, Troy patted my shoulder. "Trace, don't be too hard on yourself. Jimmy had his own way of doing things. You should know that. The man was relentless."

I released a frustrated breath, my hands forming into tight knots. "Yeah, but something tells me there's more to this than meets the eye. I think Jimmy got too close to the truth. The scrap of paper he gave me indicates he was on to something. We'll never know now."

Troy called the dispatcher. Thirty minutes later the CSI unit arrived and began the meticulous process of collecting physical evidence. The medical examiner also arrived and determined the cause and time of death. It was pretty obvious. One shot to the chest. He suffered for a short time before succumbing. Specialists took measurements and angles to determine where the shot was fired from. The single casing came from a .45 caliber weapon. They swabbed it for fingerprints.

By the time we'd finished filling out paperwork, the sun was barely higher than the mountains. My stomach growled. "You interested in a decent breakfast?"

Troy checked the time.

It was six-fifteen in the morning.

"Look, Trace, if it's okay with you, I'm going to head home and crash. I'm beat."

So was I, but I was too keyed up to sleep. After dropping me off at the precinct, we parted company with the promise to connect later that day after we'd gotten some rest and food. Not particularly in that order.

The restaurant I'd chosen served a decent breakfast and a great cup of coffee.

Sitting alone in the booth, I reviewed everything I'd learned so far. It wasn't much. Someone killed Rosa Tampico and Father O'Leary. They robbed his safe after killing him. Then someone entered Antonio's house and killed him leaving only an old newspaper as evidence. Now with Jimmy dead, my list of potential suspects was thinning. What was the connection? Who stood to gain the most by killing these people? There was only one person in my mind who could possibly benefit from these deaths … Governor Rafael Edwardo Sanchez.

Three cups of coffee and a big breakfast later, I parked my Renault in its assigned slot and got out. To my surprise, Lily's Infinity Q60 coupe was in its slot.

Interesting.

Being as quiet as possible, I entered the condo and headed to bed. Unfortunately, Wag had taken my place. He let out a low growl as I shoved him aside. At least the bed was warm.

Chapter Thirty-Four

A single shaft of light pierced through the blinds striking Lily directly in the face.

She rolled over and squinted at the clock.

It was eight o'clock. Reluctantly, Lily crawled out from under the covers. She longed for the days when she could sleep in on a Saturday morning, but those days were long gone.

After showering and blow drying her hair, she tugged on a pair of tights and a loose top. Jamming her feet into a pair of tennis shoes, she scuffed down the hall past her dad's bedroom.

Loud snoring told her he'd returned. Not wanting to disturb him, she left a note for him to call her as soon as he woke up. She placed it where she knew he'd find it … next to the coffee pot.

***

By 8:45 a.m., Lily scarfed down a bagel with cream cheese along with a glass of orange juice.

After placing the dirty dishes in the dishwasher, she shrugged on her coat and left. She reached the campus without incident, but that didn't keep her from checking her rear-view mirror every few blocks.

Because so many of her classmates had spent the night of partying, and she had the campus parking lot to herself. Only a group of students in the BSU, the Baptist Student Union were out playing a scrimmage football game with the Latter Day Saints students. It looked like the Baptists were winning.

She pulled into one of the many empty slots, got out and made her way up the steps to her dorm. No sign of anyone following her. For that, she was glad.

She intended on using her morning to catch up on her laundry, a task she'd been avoiding all week. Three loads later, she slumped into an uncomfortable chair and waited for her last load to dry. Meanwhile, she caught herself staring out the window doodling Gill's name followed by hers. She felt like a junior high school girl, but it didn't matter.

Outside, a swirl of wind caught the colored leaves and scattered them against the pane of glass startling her back to reality. She blinked and caught her breath. The room shifted, and she grabbed the window sill. It had been a while since her last treatment, and the doctors were after her to get an appointment.

Although the effects were minimal, having to leave her studies for an extended weekend in the hospital didn't fit her plans. Not as long as Gill was interested.

Her phone pinged, and she glanced at it. It was a text from Gill asking her to meet him.

Where? She texted him back.

Coffee shop next to lib.

Be there in ten.

That was all the motivation she needed. She quickly folded the last of her clothes, jammed them into the laundry basket and dashed back to her room. When she entered, she found her roommate flopped across the bed sleeping soundly. Mikala had been gone all night, and she hoped she'd not done something stupid, but her roommate wasn't the most cautious girl on campus.

She stowed her clothes in the dresser and backed out of the room without disturbing Mikala. After closing the door, she pranced down the stairs to the street level. It was going to be a fun afternoon.

***

"Hey, Lily."

Hearing her name, she slowed her pace.

It was Troy.

"What are you doing here?" She gave him her best fake smile.

Troy's face contorted. "I've been all over the campus looking for the coffee shop."

"Oh, yeah, well, I'm sorry about missing you last night. You look beat."

Jamming his hands in his pockets, he continued, "Yeah, late night. I kinda got tied up myself. I thought you'd be mad because I stood you up. Your dad and I had an emergency call we had to respond to. I'd like to make it up to you this morning."

Lily fought to control her mixed feelings. Yes, she still liked him. But hooking up with a detective would be like dating her dad. The guy worked all the time and she knew she would always be playing second fiddle to his schedule. And second fiddle was one instrument she had no intention of learning.

Brushing her hair aside, she toed the sidewalk. "Yeah, well, it wasn't actually a date, not strictly speaking. I kinda figured you'd not show. You're being so busy and all."

Troy tried to hide his disappointment. Rocking back on his heels, he pulled a hand from his pocket. "You're right. I've been pretty busy. I don't have much of a personal life. But that's going to change. With the investigation stalled, well, I've got some time on my hands. So, you want to get a cup of coffee?" It was only partially true. His chief had him on desk duty.

Lily did an abrupt about-face and started walking. "See, that's what I mean. Your investigation is stalled and so you have time for me." She hated the way her frustration spilled out, but there it was, she's said it.

Skipping to catch up, Troy took her hand in his. "I don't care how demanding my job is, I'll always have time for you."

"Yeah, right."

"I mean it."

"Okay, okay." Clutching her empty stomach, she quickened her pace. "I'm hungry, add an Orange Cranberry muffin to my breakfast, and maybe I'll let you off the hook, this time."

"Deal."

They walked in silence the rest of the way, each wrestling with their own thoughts. His, the case, hers … Gill.

***

When they reached the library door, Troy grabbed the door handle and swung it open.

A wave of laughter spilled out. Turning, Lily glanced over her shoulder. "I should have warned you. This isn't your typical library setting."

Troy cupped his ear as the noise level increased. "Say no more. It reminds me of my college days. It's all too familiar."

Lily weaved between clusters of red-eyed students, found an empty table and got seated. Leaning close, Troy caught a whiff of her cologne. His heart stuttered, and he had to force his lungs to work. It had been weeks since he had spent time with Lily, and he had forgotten how much she moved him. His eyes locked on hers.

"Troy?"

He blinked. "Oh, sorry, what's your pleasure, I'm buying," reaching for his wallet.

"I'm dying for a coffee Grande and an Orange Cranberry muffin. Oh, and ask them to warm it."

As he stepped toward the counter, Gill's imposing frame parted the crowd. His eyes switched between Lily and Troy. "Oh hey, Lily, fancy meeting you here."

Troy caught a flicker of excitement brighten Lily's face.

"Gill, what a surprise. What are you doing here?" Her voice wavered. Palms down, she tried to quell the situation before it escalated.

"Yeah, well, I thought I'd hang out here and chill. Who's this?" eying Troy warily.

Troy held his gaze without backing up.

Taking a quick step, she moved between them. "Hmm, Troy, this is Gill. He's majoring in architecture."

Gill extended his hand. "Nice to meet you, dude."

Troy forced a smile. "Nice to meet you, dude. So I guess one day when you grow up, you'll be a concrete truck driver."

"Troy!" Lily spat, "you have no right talking to Gill that way," she huffed, her fists in tight knots.

Hands held in surrender, Troy stepped back. "Hey, I was just joking—"

Lily's cell chirped interrupting the gathering conflict.

***

It was her dad.

"Sorry, I got to get this." She stepped to a quieter corner of the room. "Hey, Dad."

"Hey to you. Your note sounded urgent. What's up?"

His call couldn't have come at a worse time. Torn between telling her dad about Carnes and keeping those two knuckleheads apart, Lily made a choice. "Did you know Mr. Carnes was my grandfather?"

Silence.

"Dad?"

"No … in the two short years your mother and I were married she never mentioned it. I do remember, however, the way she looked at him that night. There was real animosity between them."

"Yeah, well, he told me about that. Look, I have a situation I need to deal with, so I gotta scoot, but Mr.

Carnes, I mean, Grandpa Carnes gave me a number for you to call … said he really needed to talk to you."

After rattling off the number, she ended the call and returned to find the two guys laughing.

"—so there I was, facing a rattlesnake with my … " Troy's face reddened as he let his story fade into the background.

"Don't quit on my account," Lily said, eyeing the two over-grown boys.

Gill grinned sheepishly. "That same thing happened to my uncle, Gov— I mean, my uncle."

Troy's eyes narrowed. Despite the notable size difference, Troy didn't seem intimidated by Gill. "What did you say your uncle's name is?"

The air suddenly grew tense and Gill looked for the exit. "Uh look, I just remembered I left my iPad in the Jeep. I gotta go." Turning, he headed for the nearest exit.

She knuckled her hips and huffed. "There you go, letting your detective side ruin everything."

"Lily, I'm sorry if I offended your friend. I was just."

Stomping her foot, Lily vented. "You were just trying to scare him off. That's what you were doing. Showing him how manly you are." Her voice deepened. "I saw how you two gripped each other. It was like two Billy-goats butting heads."

One of the things Troy admired about her was her perception. She nailed him. It was true. He didn't like his competition, and Gill was his competition.

Troy took a seat across from her. "Okay, I apologize. I was wrong, will you forgive me?"

Lily blew out a pent-up breath. It was hard for her to

stay mad at Troy, even if he'd ruined all her plans.

"Well, okay," her voice wobbled and a tear eeked from the corners of her eyes. She dabbed it with the corner of a napkin.

"Still interested in a cup of coffee?"

A sigh.

"Make it a double espresso. I think I'm going to need it."

Chapter Thirty-Five

After the disastrous Saturday, Lily was in no mood to go to church.

She couldn't believe how quickly the time had passed. It had only been four weeks since her first encounter with Gill, and yet he had turned her world upside down. Standing in front of the mirror, she recoiled at the dark circles under her eyes. What did he even see in me? She asked herself. The extra layer of make-up did little to mask the stress she was feeling.

She parked her car in a visitor's slot, got out and shuddered. The brisk wind sliced through her thin coat making her wish she'd dressed for comfort rather than fashion. Tugging her coat tighter, she made for the door where her dad waited.

Having agreed to let her sleep, Trace had gotten up and came to Sunday School. They'd arranged to rendezvous at the front door.

She gave him a quick peck on the cheek and stepped inside. He looked more worn than she'd seen him and wondered if he was working on the same case as Troy.

"Hey, Dad. Sorry I missed you last night. So, did you call Grampa Carnes?"

"I did."

"What'd he say?"

Trace's smile faded. "The man is scared to death. He's afraid he's going to be arrested and charged with Antonio's murder."

Lily felt the blood drain from her face. "Murdered?" Her words squeaked out.

"Sorry, this is no time to be talking about—"

"—Are you and Troy working on the same case?"

The lines on his face deepened. "Same one and it isn't pretty."

"Do I feel like a jerk. Yesterday, I treated Troy like pond scum for missing a date we had. Now I'm finding out he's … you're—"

The two fell into silence as they entered the foyer. After being greeted by an overly friendly lady greeter, they took their seats halfway down the aisle.

"Better watch out for that one," Lily said, a half smile tugging up the corners of her lips.

"Not to worry, she comes across a bit desperate."

The music began, and the two joined in.

Lily had only half listened to the sermon. Her mind kept wandering between the news of Antonio's murder, the news that she had a grandfather, and Gill. The few notes she'd taken were jumbled and disjointed. In frustration, she closed her bulletin and tried to listen.

It didn't work.

Mercifully, the preacher brought his message to an end, and the crowd stood to leave. As she and her dad made their way to the exit, the pastor waited to give them a departing blessing.

Lily wasn't interested in any parting blessing. She simply wanted out.

As she moved through the crowd, she heard her dad saying, "Thank you, Pastor. That was a wonderful sermon."

She parroted the words and kept going. *What did he preach about, anyway?* Her mind fluttered like a moth to a flame. Lifting the bulletin, she noticed the notes she had scribbled. *Oh yes, something about not bringing peace on earth, rather, he came to set a man against his father, a daughter against her mother.* Whatever.

***

I finished extricating myself from the overly-friendly greeter and caught a glimpse of Lily as she exited the building.

Head down, she plodded along the sidewalk, deep in thought.

Zigzagging through the crowd, I caught up to her and took her hand. "A penny for your thoughts."

She glanced up, her eyes barely holding back her tears. "So, if Jesus came to divide people, He's no different than most religious leaders who say their way is the only way."

Her abrupt assessment of the sermon caught me off guard. I did my best to keep my tone conversational. "That's only partially true."

"How so?"

I could tell she really wanted to know. Part of me wanted to take her back to the pastor and let him explain himself, but I feared I'd run into that greeter again.

"The context of that passage makes it clear that Jesus

was making a comparison between our love for Him and our love for our family. This is part of the Beatitudes where Jesus is teaching the people about a new relationship between God and man.

He went on to say, 'He who loves his family more than me is not worthy of me. And he who does not take his cross, and follows me, is not worthy of me. He who finds his life shall lose it: and he who loses his life for my sake shall find it, and he who receives me receives Him that sent me."

"So, what does it mean to be worthy of me?"

I wished I'd taken better notes. Truth was, I'd only half listened. The activity of the past weeks battled for my attention. I did my best to answer her question. "When you realize who it was that was speaking, that this was the Messiah, the promised one, His worth skyrockets. To receive Him in your heart is the same as receiving the Heavenly Father." I was on a roll now.

She took a few tentative steps along the sidewalk. Her lips pursed, her eyes fixed on a distant object. "So, do you love me more than God?"

Talk about a kick to the gut. I stopped walking and stared into her eyes. I'd never thought about that. Of course I loved her. I would do anything for her. It took me a moment to recover. Finally, I found my voice. "Again, it's a matter of comparison. When I think about what Jesus did for me on Calvary, bleeding, dying, paying my sin debt, I'd have to say my love for Him exceeds my natural love for anything."

"Including me?"

"Yeah."

"And Cami?"

"Yes."

She mulled that over for a minute.

When she spoke, it was in a whisper. "That makes sense. But how do you love someone you've never seen?"

The next thought just came to me, and I said. "They hated me without a cause."

"Say what?"

"It's a verse in the Bible. The Jews hated Jesus for no reason. It's kinda like your feelings toward me after your mother died."

Lily's lower lip trembled. "Yeah," she swiped at her tears, "I see your point. If I could hate you before I knew you, I certainly could love God without—" she paused. "That's what's been missing. God loved me knowing how rotten I am. How could I not love Him back?"

I directed our steps toward a concrete bench.

We sat.

After a moment, I took her hand. "Do you want to pray?"

She smiled through her tears. "I just did. I told God how sorry I was for hating you, for hating Him for taking mom and for all the rotten things I've done. It was as if He spoke directly to me like He spoke to that woman who they caught in adultery. He said, 'go and sin no more.'"

Chapter Thirty-Six

We stood, and she pulled me into a tight embrace.

"I think I understand. I love God. He loves me, but I love you as much as possible."

It wasn't her most poetic statement, but it was heartfelt.

All at once, a well-dressed young man stopped next to us.

"Gill, what are you doing here?" Lily sounded sincere. After the disaster in the library between him and Troy, she figured she'd never see him again.

His lips parted into a grin. "I was sitting close to the front and didn't see you until now. Why else would I come to a Protestant church?"

Hand to her chest, Lily staggered back. Bumping into her dad, she gripped his arm. "Oh, hey, this is my dad, Trace O'Reilly."

Gill's face suddenly grew tense. "Nice to meet you, sir." He accepted Trace's hand, and they eyed each other.

"So you're the nice guy Lily's been bragging about."

The color in Gill's cheeks darkened. He shrugged one shoulder. "She's a great gal, who wouldn't want to get to know her."

"I didn't think you'd want to see me again after the

way Troy treated you," Lily interjected trying to divert the conversation.

He waved the comment aside. "I'm kinda used to being treated like that, or worse. Some of the schools I attended were nothing more than reformatories. So I've built up a resistance to jerks."

Lily's mouth fell open, then snapped shut. She knew Troy wasn't a jerk, though at times he acted like one, like yesterday.

Feeling like a third wheel, I said, "Hey, look, I've got a few calls to make. Would you excuse me?" trying to give the two young people some space. Gill's Jeep Renegade was double-parked near the front door, and he motioned in its direction. Which struck me as a bit odd, but I didn't say anything.

***

"Are you hungry? I'm famished," Gill asked, opening his car door.

Lily paused at the side of the car.

"Think your dad would mind if I took you to lunch?"

She gave him a quick glance, caught his attention, and he gave her a thumbs up.

Lily brushed a few strands of hair behind her ear and smiled. "Yeah, he's cool with it, as long as I get back to campus in time to prep for my Sociology test."

A golden ray glistened off her diamond earrings, catching his attention. He reached out and touched it. "Those are beautiful. Where did you get them?"

Smiling, Lily searched the ground. "Umm, they were

a gift," not wanting to tell him they were from Troy.

Feeling the warmth of his hand so close to her skin, made her heart flutter. Forcing air into her lungs, she willed herself to breathe. "Maybe we should go." She hated breaking the moment.

Gill pulled his hand back and went around to open her door. "Do you think they mind if you leave your car?"

The question took Lily a moment. "I'll follow you. I'd hate to have someone steal it."

His face softened. "Okay, cool, you have a favorite restaurant?"

Lily's forehead wrinkled. She and Troy had their favorite places, but she wasn't about to mention them. Scrambling for an answer, she blurted, "How about Applebees's?"

Finger to his chin, he considered his options. "I'd rather Five Guys? I've heard their burgers are the bomb."

The idea pleased Lily. "Okay, I'll meet you there."

Ten minutes later, they walked into the restaurant. As they entered, he slipped his arm around her waist. The move caused a wave of warmth to radiate through her body.

Once seated, they placed their order with the waiter. "I want mine full animal style." Meaning it has mustard fried into the patty, and it comes with extra spread and grilled onions.

Not to be outdone, Gill said, "Hey dude, I'm going 3 by 3 ... three beef patties all the way."

Lily's stomach growled, and she stifled a chuckle. To break the tension, she asked, "So, Gill, what did you think of the sermon?"

He stroked the three-day stubble which defined his strong jaw line. Having only arrived near the end of the sermon, he said vaguely, "Well, it was cool. A lot different than the homilies I'm used to, but cool."

"Different? In what way?"

"Well, for starters, the priest speaks in Latin, and the English is projected on a screen behind him."

Lily nodded, trying to imagine the scene.

"And most of the time he talks about one of the Beatitudes or a Psalm. He says God is love, and that we should love each other and do the best we can. Things like that. But most of what your priest said didn't make much sense."

Lily bristled, but said nothing. Embarrassed she had paid so little attention to his message, she waited for Gill to continue.

"That part about taking up your cross and carrying it reminded me of those people down in Brazil, who actually get themselves crucified. Is that what he's suggesting?"

Shifting uncomfortably, Lily racked her brain. "Umm, I think he was speaking metaphorically. It means giving your life completely to Jesus Christ." she added softly, playing with her water glass.

Gill drew a sharp breath. "What's that got to do with anything? I don't think the preacher should be telling people who they should believe in," he huffed. "That's the thing I don't like about religion. They're always trying to control your life using scare tactics." As he spoke, he became more agitated. "If you don't do as we say you'll go to Hell," he mocked.

Lily's stomach knotted.

He continued, "Actually, this whole church thing seems a bit hypocritical. Everybody dresses up and puts on their Sunday smile as if everything is *fine*, but inside, they're dying." His voice grew more intense as he spoke.

Lily forced down a swig of water.

"And furthermore, what business is it of theirs what we do with our lives. As long as we don't hurt anybody and do the best we can, it will all work out in the end. My priest says God wouldn't send anybody to Hell, if you've done your best." By now, his face had turned a deep crimson and the veins in his neck throbbed.

Their food arrived. He leaned back and took a calming breath.

The air between them grew tense. Before she could offer a prayer, she watched him plow into his sandwich. She wiped her sweaty palms on her pants. "Gill, maybe we should talk about this later. I don't want religion to spoil our dinner."

He nodded and washed down a mouthful of fries with his coke. "You know Lily, I like being around you. We seem to be cut from the same cloth." His voice grew soft.

She felt the same way. They were kindred spirits, but she wanted it to be more … way more.

Chapter Thirty-Seven

The front door slammed sending a shockwave through the condo.

Wag leapt from the couch and growled.

I had fallen asleep halfway through the football game. Hearing the door slam, I jolted to life. Gawking, I watched Lily stomp across the floor and into her room.

"Have a nice time at dinner?"

"Grrr!"

I knew it was best to leave things alone.

A few minutes later, Lily returned to the living room, dressed in jeans and a flannel shirt. She plopped down next to me and crossed her arms. Letting out a frustrated huff, she brought me up to speed with Gill.

Finally, after she exhausted her emotions. I took her hand in mine and kissed it. "You know Lily, this guy, if he really cares for you he will want to know where you stand on the important matters such as your convictions, your beliefs. If he wants to have a relationship with you, he needs to talk to me. Let me get to know him. I'm not such a bad guy … am I?"

Lily fought off a weak smile. "No, you're not so bad; once you get past your dog, your gun and your reputation."

"What about Troy, except for having a dog, he has a

gun and a reputation. Where does he fit into the picture?"

Swallowing the lump in her throat, Lily looked up, moisture glistened on her eyes lashes; she splashed them away with a blink. "Oh Daddy, at times I could shoot him. He showed up at the worst possible time and ruined everything." Tears rolled down her cheeks, unhindered.

Caught between Lily and my friend, I pulled her close. I knew Troy was a good man. But Gill? … I'd only met him once and not had time to form an opinion of him. On the other hand, when it came to matters of the heart, I was a lousy counselor. My track record of love and marriage was riddled with holes. "Just go slow, and let God have a chance to change his heart … and yours."

That seemed to have settled the matter until her phone buzzed.

It was Gill.

***

As Lily headed for her room, my cell phone jangled.

I dreaded looking at the caller ID. I knew crime didn't take a day off, but crime investigators did. Smiling, I answered the phone.

"Hey, stranger." Cami's voice was a welcomed sound. "Busy?"

"Nah, just chillin'. You in town?"

"Yeah. The governor is taking a few days off. He sent his staff home. You hungry?"

"I thought you'd never ask. Let's meet at Swabbies."

Cami released a sultry chuckle. "I've been sitting here for the last ten minutes. You'd better hurry or one of those guys across the restaurant might start hitting on me.”

“I’ll be there in twenty minutes, depending on the traffic.”

***

The veranda outside of Swabbies on the River was the perfect spot to relax on a Sunday evening.

Sitting beneath sixty-foot shade trees, Cami and I stared at the Sacramento River. A fish jumped, catching a dragonfly in its mouth and splashed back into the lazy swirls. The slow movement of its current reflected the late-afternoon sun making it shimmer with rays of gold and orange. Soft music filled the silence and low conversations in hushed tones carried through the crisp air.

After catching Cami up on the most recent developments in the case, and Lily’s guy troubles, I sank into a blue funk.

“Why so glum?” Cami asked.

The sun hung low on the horizon. After my conversation with Lily, it was my turn to have my heart tested. I lifted my glass of iced tea, took a sip and cleared my throat. “I was just thinking how nice it is to be sitting at dinner with the one woman who really understands me and doesn’t run away.”

Cami patted my arm. “Trace, you’re such a romantic. But you have a selective memory. Aren’t you forgetting I left you because of your drinking, and your job? You were a walking disaster, and I didn’t want you to pull me down with you.”

I searched her eyes. It was true. I was both a workaholic and an alcoholic. My marriage with Monica was a disaster as well. The only good to come out of it was Lily … and her brother. I had to hit rock bottom for God to get my attention. Now that Cami and I were believers, it was time for us to start over. At least, that's what I hoped.

I took Cami's hand. It was warm and soft. Her fingers wrapped around mine, and I gave them a reassuring squeeze. "How about after the election when your life slows down, and this crazy case wraps up, we sit down and do some serious planning?"

Wrinkling her nose, Cami tucked a strand of hair behind her ear. "If that was a proposal you're got to do better." An impish twinkle danced in her eye.

I felt heat creep up my neck. "No, Cami, that was not a proposal, but if you want—"

Her phone vibrated. Lifting her finger, she silenced me.

"Hello?"

I waited, not trying to listen to the one-sided conversation.

"Having dinner."

Her eyes rounded as she stared at me. My heart stuttered.

"With Trace, I told you." Frustration soaked every word. "No, sir, that's been handled. I—"

She picked up her fork and stabbed the last bite of potato and stuck it into her mouth and chewed.

"As I said, it's been handled—"

I watched steam escape from her ears.

"All right, I'll take care of it tomorrow—"

She swallowed and took a sip of tea.

"Now?" she huffed. "Okay, I'll handle it." She mashed the red button as if it were a roach. "Sometimes I think that man is crazy."

I mirrored Cami's action as she stood. "Who, the governor?"

"No, I mean, yes. That was his chief of staff. But I'd bet the governor put him up to it. He wants me to call the police chief and remind him about a certain federal grant that could evaporate if the investigation doesn't go away."

My pulse quickened. "That's obstruction of justice," I blurted.

Cami remained silent as I held her coat. She slid her arms into its sleeves and faced me.

"I know, but what can I do? If I speak up, he'll ruin my career."

"Sounds like a strong arm tactic. Will it work? I mean, will the chief cave?"

She took a step toward her car. "He will. He always has."

Being a veteran of the Sacramento Police Department, I knew she was right. I opened her door and helped her in.

Turning the key, she huffed.

"What's wrong?"

"Stupid me, I left my lights on, and the battery is dead."

"Want me to call AAA?"

She shook her head. "No, this is a company car and

the gov doesn't have it."

I didn't carry jumper cables, so offering her a jump was out of the question. "Okay, how about I go and pick up a jumper cable and come back. We'll have you on your way in a few minutes."

"That's okay. But I don't want to be left here alone. I'll go with you, it's the least I can do."

The thought of hanging out with Cami even to run to Walmart lifted my spirits. "Hop in, but no complaints. This car is a real classic."

She grimaced, got in and clicked the seat belt.

"Before we do that, do you mind if we run by campaign headquarters. I need to pick up some papers."

The longer I'm with you, the better, I mused. With a nod, I eased my car into traffic and headed across town. As we crossed N. St. Viaduct Street, a semi pulled to an abrupt stop halfway across the bridge blocking traffic.

I glanced into my rear view mirror and cringed. "Brace yourself." A moment later, a dump truck slammed into my car.

Cami's cries were drowned out by the crunch of twisting metal and squealing tires. The force of the impact drove us into the guardrail. Support wires holding up the aging bridge snapped. My crumpled Renault slid sideways toward the tipping point.

"Trace, we gotta get out of here," she hollered, her eyes wide.

Gripping the steering wheel, I fought to hold the brake. "I know, but my door is stuck."

Struggling with the handle, Cami's voice tensed. "So is mine."

Seconds stretched.

"Kick out the window."

Cami scooted around and kicked. The window shattered.

"Get out, now!" I shouted as the car inched closer to the edge.

"What about you?"

"No time—"

Chapter Thirty-Eight

ami shimmied out, fell on the concrete and rolled out of the way.

Sparks flew as the rumpled Renault crashed over the railing. Hand to her mouth, Cami watched in horror as my car, and I plunged into the icy waters of the Sacramento River.

"Trace," she called, tears staining her vision.

"Someone call 9-1-1," a bystander hollered.

Cami gasped as bubbles percolated on the water's surface. Stripping off her coat, she kicked off her shoes, and prepared to jump in."

"Hey lady, you don't want to do that," someone hollered.

"Yes, I do. That's my fiancé down there." Turning, she leaped over the edge and into the rushing current.

***

Amidst swirling water and debris, I fought to hold my breath.

My seat belt refused to release its grip. Time was running out. My lungs screamed for oxygen but I knew to yield would be fatal. Frantically, I searched for anything that I could use to cut the restraint. Inside the glove compartment, lay a pocket knife. I grabbed it and began to slice at the restraint, but the dull blade did little.

This was not good.

Not at all.

Time and oxygen were running out. In the ceiling, a pocket of air bobbed and swayed with the movement of the car. Straining, I sucked it in, buying myself a few precious moments. Blindly, I tried again to cut the seatbelt. Progress was slow, and my strength was fading.

It was a race against time.

The urge to expel my spent oxygen and inhale was palpable, but I knew to do so would be fatal. My hands weakened, and I felt myself drifting. "Oh God, help me."

Darkness.

I'd been here before.

Dying wasn't so bad.

I'd be home soon.

***

Kicking against the chilly current, Cami followed the plume of bubbles down to the car.

Amazingly, it landed on its all fours with Trace frantically struggling with his seatbelt.

After coming up for another breath, Cami dove again while onlookers on the bridge cheered. Something bumped into her leg, and she fought to keep from screaming. It was a bloated dead fish. Relieved, she thanked the Lord it wasn't Trace. Fingers splayed like a spider web, she searched wildly for the wounded Renault. Her hair swirled in front of her, obscuring her vision.

Suddenly, her hand found the front door.

She yanked.

It resisted.

Her lungs protested, yet she knew what she had to do. Lifting her foot, she kicked the windshield.

It splintered. Tugging it back, she peered through murky water, Trace's head bobbed lifelessly. "Oh God, no."

Her heart sputtered.

Grabbing him by the shirt, she tugged.

Something resisted.

It was the seatbelt. With her strength nearly gone, she gave it a quick jerk.

It snapped, releasing its hold.

She grabbed Trace by his coat and pulled him free. Giving the roof a powerful kick, she lunged upward. A moment later, she came up gasping.

A cheer rose from the onlookers, but the celebration was short-lived. She dragged Trace's lifeless body to the river bank. Seconds ticked, as she began pounding on his chest. Rolling him over, she pressed on his back and worked his elbows like a pump. Then, she rolled him over, cleared his throat and began mouth to mouth resuscitation.

Time hung in the balance as she fought to save him. Suddenly, Trace coughed. Struggling for a breath, he sat up, gasping.

"Oh Trace," Cami threw her arms around him.

His body began to tremble as shock set in. "Cami," he sputtered. "It was so beautiful."

Pulling back, Cami swiped the water from her eyes

and gaped at him. "What was?"

He cleared his throat and took a deep breath. "Heaven."

***

"Any news about the other driver?"

Troy hovered over me since I'd been admitted to the hospital.

"Only that he was dead when he hit us. The poor guy had a coronary and lost control," I said.

"Yeah, but isn't it a bit odd. First, the semi stops, then this guy in a truck rams you?" Cami asked, her hair and clothes still damp.

Lily burst into the hospital recovery room, eyed Troy, then turned her attention to her dad. "Daddy, I was so worried about you. You gonna be okay?"

Taking her into my arm, I gave her a soggy hug. "I am now that you're here. But I will admit, it was a close one." Clearing my throat, I added, "Did Cami tell you I caught a glimpse of Heaven?"

Hand to her mouth, Lily sucked in a sharp breath. "No,—"

"I'm sorry Honey," Cami cut in, "I didn't want to worry you."

I raised my hand. The IV tube followed my movements. "That's okay. I was only there for a few seconds, but it felt like a lifetime. I heard Cami crying out to God."

Cami leaned over and placed a warm kiss on my lips. "Well, I did some serious praying. I'm certainly glad God was listening. Now, how about we take you home," she said, patting my arm.

The doctor entered drawing everyone's attention. "How about it doc? Can you release me into this woman's care?"

He lifted the chart, scanned it and looked up. "Your lungs are clear, and there seems to be no neurological or brain damage—"

"Oh, he had brain damage all right," Troy chirped. "You're forgetting he's a private eye."

Lily glared.

Cami smiled.

I chuckled under my breath.

"Well, as I was saying, if you're feeling up to it, I think I can release you into your own recognizance."

That was the best news I'd heard since coming here. Pushing back the dinner tray, I sat up. "Great, we've still got suspects to interview—"

"Oh no you don't," Cami and Lily said in unison.

"You need to take your medication, and get a good night's sleep," Lily insisted.

I was outnumbered and outgunned.

It felt good.

With Troy's help, I climbed into a wheelchair. "You'll have to hold the fort without my expertise."

"I'll get by," Troy kidded.

Chapter Thirty-Nine

Golden rays spilled through the curtains into my bedroom and leaked onto a small spot on the hardwood floor.

I yanked the sheets over my head and released a frustrated sigh. *Why did the sun have to come up so early?*

Heavy breathing preceded a large black nose as Wag pushed under the covers bumping against my leg, jolting me to life.

"Wag, don't you know to knock?"

He leaped upon the bed and panted in my face.

"I take it Lily's gone, leaving me with the job of walking you. Don't you know I'm convalescing?"

Ignoring my complaint, Wag jumped from the bed and scampered to the door.

Still muttering, I jerked on a pair of sweatpants, laced on a pair of tennis shoes and clipped the leash to Wag's collar.

One look at the clock and I knew why Wag was so anxious for a run. It was nearly four in the afternoon. Oh well, the run would do me good as well as clear my lungs. By the time I returned, I was chomping at the bit to pick up where I'd left off. Since opening my office, my phone hadn't stopped ringing with potential clients.

Several looked promising and I was planning on bringing them in for an interview when my phone vibrated.

"Hello?"

"Trace?"

"Who did you expect?"

"I thought Cami or Lily might be there. You're supposed to be convalescing."

"I am, but Wag didn't get the memo. What's up?"

Troy moved the phone to th other ear. "With you out of commission and me on desk duty, I've had time to think."

"And?"

"And I think we need to take a fresh look at things."

"How did your interview with the governor go?

"It didn't. His attorney must be getting paid a pile of money because he threw every roadblock he could think of in my way. He's even threatening to withhold funding for the new police cruisers. The chief is still livid with me for getting a judge to issue a bench warrant. If I don't come up with some solid evidence quick, I'll be joining you in private practice."

Taking a seat on a kitchen stool, I tugged Wag back from the door. "All right, what do you want me to do?"

"Can I come over, and let you take a look at everything. Maybe I'm missing something."

"Yeah sure and bring a box of donuts and coffee. I'm starving, and my refrigerator is empty."

The call ended.

Someone knocked on the front door.

Wag jumped and began barking and scratching on it.

"Hold on Wag," I said, shoving him back.

I unlocked the three deadbolts, slid the bolt back and swung the door open. Troy stood, a box of donuts in one hand and his phone in the other. "May I come in?"

A smile tugged at the corners of his mouth as I stepped aside.

"Take a seat while I fill Wag's food bowl."

Troy watched in silence as I went through the routine of feeding the beast.

"Man, that dog eats more than you." I didn't appreciate his observation.

"Don't you have something better to do than compare me to Wag?"

He ignored my statement. Speaking out of the corner of his mouth, Troy said, "One thing's got me puzzled. I've got one eyewitness who insists he saw a man jump from the truck that hit you, and another who says it was just the driver. Yet, we've got a set of fingerprints off the steering wheel which doesn't match any in our database."

"Aren't they the driver's?" I asked, snatching a jelly filled donut before Troy did.

Shaking his head, Troy reached for another donut and chomped into it. He shoved it to the side of his mouth and continued, "Nope, that guy was wearing driving gloves, but here's the thing. Those were the same prints we found on the fire poker."

I felt my jaw tighten. "What? That's the first I've heard that."

Nodding. "Yeah, well some of this stuff is just now coming out." Pulling a fresh page from his notepad, he double clicked his pen and began, "Here's what we know. We've got one dead priest, Antonio Beretta lying in the morgue along with Jimmy, shot at close range, and a dead chauffeur."

"Don't forget a missing jewelry box," I added, looking over the rim of my coffee mug. "By the way, good job on the coffee."

"Thanks, coming from you, that's a real compliment."

"And then where's the two scraps of paper with matching dates, April 4th, 1992." I paused and narrowed my eyes. "Speaking of dates, how did it go with Lily? Patch things up?"

Troy washed down the last of his donut with a swig of coffee. Making a face, he said, "That's a negative. I called her last night. She said she was busy. Right in the middle of my call, someone beeped in. It was Gill."

Shaking my head, I was glad I wasn't involved in the dating game. "What can you say? The guy has good instincts."

"Yeah, he's a real charmer. But you know, he said something that got me thinking."

"What's that?" grabbing the last donut.

Closing his eyes, Troy thought back "It was a passing remark, but it went something like … 'that's what my uncle, Gov—, I mean my uncle,' he said."

I gulped. "He said my uncle, Gov—, as in Governor?"

"Yeah, I kinda got that impression."

"I didn't know Sanchez had any brothers or sisters."

Troy shoved some papers aside. "He doesn't, that's just it. I did a background search and came up empty. Then, using Heritage.com, ancestry.com, and the government database, I discovered the governor was an only child, both parents are deceased." He stopped and pulled out his iPad and did a Google search using the name Anna Sanchez. His eyes widened.

"What?"

Barely able to speak, Troy forced the words out. "It says his first wife was embroiled in a dispute over an abducted child. The report states the child went missing on April 4th, 1992."

I jumped up, knocking my chair over.

Wag jolted to life, and came to investigate.

"See, it's right here in the public record."

I leaned in closer to get a better look. By now, my neck and back ached, probably from the car wreck or the stress. "I can't believe it. That's the same day my son went missing."

"True, but if you'll remember, the hospital records were lost and when they found them, it appeared they'd been altered. The hospital took all the blame, and Sanchez was exonerated from any wrongdoing," Troy said, staring at the list of clues.

Jamming my hands in my pockets, I began to pace. "Man, this whole thing is getting deeper by the second."

Clicking his pen, Troy drew a big star next to this new information. Without looking up, he continued, "We have two sets of fingerprints, and no one to match them with. And a set of muddy footprints going in and coming from the Beretta murder scene."

"Which reminds me," I said, my finger raised. "I learned just a few days ago that Mr. Carnes is my father-in-law."

"Who told you that?" Troy's voice inched up a notch.

"He told Lily and asked her to give me a message."

Troy's smile faded. "What was the message?"

"That he didn't kill his boss, and now that he was dead, he had some compelling information, which could sink Sanchez's chances at getting elected."

Troy slumped into a chair. "And you believe him?"

"I've got no reason not to."

"Anyone else know this?"

"Only Lily," I didn't sound too convincing.

"What about that lug head, Gill? If he is indeed the governor's nephew, we've got problems."

Troy stood and twirled his pen between his fingers. "And then there is the governor. We've got his fingerprints on the bottle of Bourbon, placing him at the murder scene. But the chief strictly forbade me from doing anything involving the governor."

Rubbing my chin, I narrowed my eyes. "Yes, he did, but that doesn't mean I can't question him. I'm a private citizen, and I have every right to know where the presidential candidate stands on certain issues."

Chapter Forty

S oft moonlight filtered through the branches as the world said goodbye to a perfect day.

It had been two days since the incident involving Trace, and a dump truck and Lily decided to cut her classes to help her dad recover. However, after one day of her doting over him, he was ready to get back to work.

And she was ready for a break herself.

Fortunately, Gill came to the rescue. Rather than return to class, she found spending time with him much more interesting.

Yes indeed.

Much more interesting.

They'd spent most of the day visiting an art museum and window shopping. After a relaxing dinner, Gill walked her to his Jeep. He tossed a black leather jacket in the back seat, and closed the door. Then he came around to the driver's side.

"Where are we going?" Lily asked, gripping the door for support.

"You gotta promise me, you won't tell. I'm going to take you to my uncle's house."

Lily's eyes widened. "Why the secrecy? I thought your uncle lived up north or something."

Shaking his head, Gill's hair blew in the wind. "Nope, my uncle has several homes. This one is his residence. He has one in Washington, D.C. and a condo in Vale.

Lily brushed the hair from her eyes. "Washington? What is he, some kind of politician?"

Gill pointed at Lily, "Bingo. He's the governor."

Mouth gaping, Lily tried to hide her surprise. She'd already guessed they were connected, but to hear it from him caused her heart to flutter. "You're Governor Sanchez's nephew?"

Nodding, Gill's grin widened. "Yeah, but you gotta promise to keep it to yourself. Uncle is sensitive about it."

Lily's skin prickled with goosebumps. "I didn't realize he had any family."

"Well, he does … sorta. It's confusing. He tells me he adopted me, but most of the time I call him uncle because it keeps things simple."

Remembering the last time she saw the governor, her face clouded.

"What's wrong?"

Forcing a weak smile, she brushed a strand of hair from the corner of her mouth. "I was just thinking about the last time I saw your uncle. It was a number of years ago at Luciano's home. Back then he was just a land developer and Mr. Beretta threw a big costume party—" her throat closed as tears clouded her vision. Taking a halting breath, she continued. "That was the night my mother was killed by—" she couldn't bring herself to say it. "I still have nightmares of that night." She shuddered, then buried her face in her hands and sobbed bitterly.

Gill laid his hand on her heaving shoulders. His touch was unlike anything she'd felt before. The warmth from his hand radiated down her arms, into her chest, her lungs. It reached deep into her soul, awakening feelings long denied. She wished she could bury her head in his shoulder and let him take away all the pain, the loneliness, the memories.

"I know, I was there," his voice was raspy.

Glancing up, her breath turned cold. "You were?"

His eyes grew distant. "I sorta popped in unannounced."

Ragged memories scraped over raw wounds as visions of that night stirred within her. "I'm a bit fuzzy, I mean, it's a bit fuzzy," a loose giggle percolated in her throat, and she wondered where it came from. "I don't seem to remember you being there."

Gill turned off the main road and on to the gravel lane which led to the governor's ranch. The tree-lined road formed a narrow tunnel illuminated only by the lone vehicle's headlights. Behind it, the darkness closed in like a thick curtain.

"When we get to the house, I'll show you a picture. I think you'll be surprised," as he spoke, his hand clasped hers. She clutched it and brought it close to her chest. Her heart skipped a beat, and she felt lightheaded.

"I just can't believe all that's happened. Meeting you, learning I have a grandfather, being followed by—" Her dreamy smile faded at the mention of being followed.

Gill's curly hair glistened in the dull illumination. His muscular neck and broad shoulders held Lily's attention as she wondered what it would be like to wake each morning with her head resting next to his.

He brought the car to a gentle stop, got out and came around to the passenger's side. Like a valet attendant, he opened her car door and bowed at the waist. She took his extended hand and stepped out.

"Wow," she said, trying to take it all in.

The mansion extended beyond the lighted parking area. In the silver moonlight, she caught a glimpse of the white fence encircling the equestrian fields.

A light breeze ruffled her hair, and she took a deep breath. "I could get used to this," she sighed. "This is where you grew up?"

Shaking his head, he looked up into the velvet sky, inhaled the crisp air and let it out slowly. "No. Actually, I didn't stay here much. My uncle sent me away to private schools for most of my education. I think that was easier to explain than having me get in his way. Plus, my stepmom doesn't like me very much. She doesn't like anyone to come between her and my dad, uh, I mean, uncle." As he spoke, his voice deepened.

Taking her by the hand, Gill led her from the car.

A wave of exhilaration swept over her.

"Whoa, I'm a bit lightheaded," stabilizing herself on his arm.

"Yeah, me too, it must be the altitude."

Hand in hand, he led her past a triple gas lamp. Its amber glow illuminated the flagstone sidewalk, giving it a soft, warm appearance. They paused where a golden shaft of light made a perfect circle. Leaning down, Gill drew her into a close embrace. His lips found her lips, and they melded into one.

Her legs weakened, and he caught her. "My, that was different."

"Different good? Or different bad?"

A loose chuckle bubbled in her throat. She wasn't sure where it came from, but it felt good. "Different good."

Hand on his cheek, she pulled him close and returned the kiss. This time, she gave herself fully to it.

The heat from his body radiated through her blouse. She felt her temperature rise, and her head swim.

As his hands stroked her back and descended, she pulled away. "No, we are moving way too fast," she said, looking at her feet.

"What? Don't you love me?" his voice raspy, pulling her close.

"Of course I love you, but we can't go on like this. If you really love me, you need to talk to my dad before we get too emotionally attached."

Leaning close, he whispered, "I think we're well past that stage, don't you?"

His warm breath wafted across her neck, sending her heart into overdrive. Her steps faltered. "Whoa, there, girl … don't go passing out on me now. At least wait until I get you inside," he said, as he led her to the front door.

Lily's mind screamed in protest. She had to slow things down. "I mean it, Gill. My dad's not such a bad guy. He just wants to meet you and lay down some ground rules."

"Ground rules." His voice grew thick. "I don't understand what your father has to do with it. I'm in love with you not *him*."

Her heart did a back-flip, but she held her ground. "Well, that's my dad for you. He's sorta old fashioned that way."

Wrapping his arms around her, he tugged her close and nuzzled her neck with his nose. "I understand your dad was in an accident. Is he going to be all right?"

Shiverflesh chilled her skin. "I, I didn't know anyone knew about that. I certainly didn't tell you."

Closing the door behind him, he threw the lock and turned. "Oh, I guess I heard it on the news, something about a truck losing control."

Lily bit her lip. His cavalier personality and winning smile disarmed her. She found herself staring up into his eyes.

Chapter Forty-One

"Come, let me show you around."

Taking her hand, Gill led her deeper into the sprawling home.

As they moved from room to room, Lily's eyes widened. The updated kitchen and bathrooms gave her lots of ideas. "My head is swimming with thoughts of renovating my condo," she said, hand to her forehead.

Pulling her close, Gill's eyes held her attention. "You sure it's the house and not being near me?"

It was true. Being near him, gave her a sense of completion, of wholeness, like something missing had been found. And she found herself lost in his gaze.

"Here, let me finish giving you the tour," Gill said, breaking the trance.

After inspecting the spacious house, Gill stopped. "And this is the den," ending the tour with a grand sweep.

It was well-appointed with deeply cushioned couches and a large fireplace. With the flick of a switch, the gas jets sparked to life. Soon the room glowed with a crackling fire.

"Sit, can I get you something to drink?" he asked, stepping over to a wet-bar.

Lily's stomach clenched. She'd seen what alcohol did to her father, but she also didn't want to make Gill think she was a prude.

"Oh, nothing, I don't drink on a full stomach," patting her midsection, "but I am a bit lightheaded," she said.

Her tongue felt like cotton.

Gill shrugged and continued filling two glasses with Gin and water. "That's okay. This will settle your stomach."

His wolfish grin didn't escape her notice, but she accepted the proffered drink anyway.

Taking a seat next to her, he checked his watch for the third time. An interesting glint appeared, then vanished from his eyes.

Lily tried to concentrate, but her thoughts blurred. All she wanted was to stretch out and relax.

Pulling her close, he whispered, "It's getting late. You want to lie down?" The alcohol on his breath sucked the wind from her lungs. *Had he put something in her dinner drink? Is that why he kept checking his watch?*

Reasoning abandoned her.

This is not good, not at all.

Struggling to sit upright, Lily felt his hand on her leg. With effort, she pushed it away.

"You know I love you. Why are you holding out on me?" he said, trying to kiss her again.

Her skin felt like ants were crawling all over her. She tried to resist, but he pressed closer.

Smack!

Lily's hand stung from the force of her action, but it was the only thing she could think of doing.

He jerked back. His eyes wild, shocked.

"I, I'm sorry Gill, but you were hurting me."

Rubbing his cheek, confusion and astonishment marked his features. "I never wanted to I hurt you. It's just that," he paused and looked away. "It's just that most girls don't …"

Lily slid from his hold and gawked at him. "Don't what? You mean to say you're not a," her breath caught in her throat. "Gill, I made a vow to God not to throw my purity away. I want to give it to my husband the night of our marriage."

As sudden as a clap of thunder, his expression changed, his voice grew distant, his eyes fixed, uncertain. "You wouldn't want to marry me anyway."

The pain in his voice made Lily's heart ache. "Why Gill, why would I not want to marry you?"

He pulled away and played with his fingers. The mechanical tone of his voice sent a chill down Lily's back. "I, I've done some things . . . bad things."

Tucking a strand of hair behind her ear, Lily did her best to focus. "Gill, we all have done some things. The Bible says we have all sinned and come short of God's glory. That's what I was trying to tell you the other day. We don't have to carry a real cross because Christ did it for us. His death satisfied God's anger against us. When we place our faith in Him, we have God's peace and forgiveness of the things we've done, past, present and future."

Shaking his head, Gill continued, "You don't understand. I've done some really bad things. I've killed people."

The air in Lily's lungs escaped. "You did? When? Why?" Clutching her stomach, she said, "I think I'm going to be sick." She stood on wobbly legs, stumbled to the sink and splashed cold water on her face.

It helped.

Unblinking, he continued, "They were fighting, Mr. Beretta and my uncle. I had to do something. I ran and grabbed the poker from the fireplace. When I returned Mr. Beretta had knocked my uncle to the floor and was beating him. The next thing I saw was Mr. Beretta, lying on the floor. His head smashed in and there was blood everywhere. Gazing at his hands, he rubbed them together as if he were trying to wash off the blood.

Lily's lips trembled. "Gill, when were you at Mr. Beretta's estate?"

He held her gaze. "It was several weeks ago. I took my uncle there to meet with Mr. Beretta. He thought I was his driver, but I tricked him. I wanted to surprise him, and show him I was a good driver. Loyalty and fidelity, that's what he drilled into my head."

"Gill, was that the driver's hat and leather coat in your car?"

He nodded. "My uncle and Mr. Beretta argued . . . something about a jewelry box. Then the lights went out. It was so scary." He covered his face with his hands.

She crossed the room feeling steadier and took his hands.

Through muffled lips, he spoke again. "It's the same with that other man."

Lily's chest constricted making it hard to breathe.

Between sobs, Gill continued, "The other night I drove my uncle to a warehouse where he was supposed to meet a man. He said he wanted money, or he'd take some information to the police."

"What information?"

His fingers trembled as he pulled a bloody envelope from his coat pocket, and laid it on the coffee table.

Driven by curiosity, Lily picked it up. It was still sealed. "How did you get it?"

Numbly, he closed his eyes. "I was afraid for my uncle. I disobeyed his order and got out of the car and snuck around to the back of the building. The man had a gun pointed at my uncle, uh, my stepdad. I think he was planning to kill him. I couldn't let that happen, so I jumped him from behind. We wrestled. I knocked my head on something. The next thing I know, I'm standing over him with a gun in my hand. I guess I blacked out after I shot him." Glancing down at his hands, he rubbed them on his pants. "Blood, I can't get it off of me," he sobbed.

Lily wrapped her arms around his neck and drew him close. She wanted it to last but knew it couldn't. "Oh, Gill, I'm so sorry."

Pushing her away, he looked around, his eyes were wild. "You're just saying that. You want that envelope just like the others, but I won't let you have it." His voice turned cold.

Hand to her chest, Lily pulled away. "No Gill, it's not like that—"

With a quick move, he snatched it from her fingers and tucked it in his coat. That's when she saw it. It was a photograph of her, Mr. Sanchez and a younger version of Guillermo … Gill.

Lily scooped it up and gasped as her eyes fell on the

picture.

"Hey, give it back." He grabbed for it, but she dodged out of his reach.

Movement caught Lily's attention, and she froze.

Chapter Forty-Two

Governor Sanchez stepped into the den brandishing a revolver.

Lily's heart jolted to a stop.

"You? What are you doing here?" The governor's face darkened into a deep purple.

"I, I—"

"Uncle, I wasn't expecting you. I thought you were—"

"Shut-up, Gill. I came to clean up the mess you made of things." Then he snatched the photograph from Lily's trembling fingers.

Looking shocked, Gill stepped back. "Uncle, what are you doing with that gun?" the tone of his voice returned to normal.

"Gill, give me that envelope," the governor said. Keeping the gun trained on Lily, he extended his hand. "I told you not to get mixed up with this girl, that she was nothing but trouble. Now look what you've done. I can't believe you kissed her."

Eyes wide, Lily sucked in a sharp breath. By now, all traces of the Benadryl he'd given her were gone. "Gill, what's going on?"

Stepping closer the governor took the envelope from him. "Go ahead. Tell her. Tell her what Guillermo means in English," he snarled.

Gill's face turned a pasty white, and he slumped to the couch. "My name is Guillermo Jose Miguel Sanchez, but you can call me Willie," he said, barely above a whisper.

Hand to her throat, Lily fingered the golden necklace.

Sanchez stuffed the envelope in his coat pocket. "A lot of people died to keep my little secret. It's unfortunate you are going to join them."

"Governor, I don't understand. At least, you could tell me why."

Shifting the gun to his other hand, he looked at Lily. A sarcastic smile spread across his face. "Oh? You didn't know? Willie is your brother, the one my wife took from the hospital."

Bile crept up Lily's throat. "I can't believe I kissed my brother," she said, trying to spit.

Wobbling to his feet, Gill stood between his uncle and Lily. "But Uncle, you told me my parents were dead, that I had no family."

"Shut up *Willie*, don't say another word." Looking at Lily, he continued. "Don't believe anything he says … not the killings, not the meeting with Mr. Beretta, nothing. You see, Willie has problems. From his earliest days, he acted out delusional behavior. I guess he was bi-polar even as a child. We thought he had a vivid imagination."

"No, I didn't imagine it. I remember mother and you. You were there when she got sick. It was you who made her eat all those pills which made her fall asleep."

The governor brushed aside his statement with a

wave. "Impossible, the boy is delusional … always has been. That's why I sent him to schools for kids with special needs."

"No, Uncle it is you who is delusional. Those schools were private Catholic schools for rich kids." Willie's eyes switched between Lily and his uncle.

Looking at Gill, Lily sputtered, "I can't believe you kissed me like that. My own brother—," Lily sputtered.

The governor's hysterical laughter cut him off. He shoved Lily aside. "I tried to help you son, but you just wouldn't listen." The governor's tone dripped with cynicism.

Lily watched the interplay between the two and wondered who was telling the truth and who wasn't. "But what about that envelope Gill? How did you get it?" she demanded.

Moving closer, the governor shifted his weight. "Willie, don't say another word. You have already said too much. You've spoiled everything." With the wave of the gun, he pointed to the front of the house. "It's time we get going."

Gill faced his uncle, "Going? Going where?"

Sanchez shoved the gun into his ribs. "Don't ask questions. Just get into the car."

With their hands raised, they began to walk.

"What are you going to do with us?" Lily asked, trying to think of a way to slow things down.

Nothing worked.

Time was running out.

Oh Lord … help us!

Chapter Forty-Three

The governor's tone grew sarcastic.

He opened the car door. "I'm sorry to inform you, but you two are going to have an unfortunate accident. It wasn't what I'd originally planned, but plans change." Looking at Lily, he continued, "You should count yourself a lucky girl. You weren't supposed to live this long, but you did, thanks to Dr. Peterson."

At the mention of his name, Lily's breath turned cold. She hated that man for what he had done to her. On the other hand, he did save her life, but at this moment, gratitude was the last thing on her mind; surviving another day was.

"Now, it looks like I'll have to take matters into my own hands. Get in," he said, flashing the weapon.

"But Uncle, all I ever wanted to do was make you proud of me. That's why I killed those evil men."

Sanchez sneered and backhanded him. "You didn't kill those men, you fool. You were too weak. You dropped that poker just close enough for me to reach it. I did the rest. As far as killing Jimmy, I knew it was you who drove me to the warehouse. And I knew you would try to stop him. But again, you just stood there like a stupid idiot. I did the dirty work.

"What happened to your regular driver? Didn't he

know what you were doing?" Lily asked, stalling for time.

The governor let out a mirthless chuckle. "Yeah, well, Larry knew too much. I had to eliminate him." Looking at Gill, the governor continued. "The only fly in the ointment was you, you big dummy. You must have overheard the conversation with my chief of staff when I ordered him to call Cami back to campaign headquarters. You just about blew it by leaving your fingerprints on the steering wheel of that dump truck."

Gill's shoulders slumped, and he swallowed hard. "I was just trying to make you proud."

Lily's eyes burned. "You'll never get away with this. The police are on their way right now," Lily said, hoping to throw Sanchez off balance.

Before Lily could duck, the governor swung.

Smack!

The impact jerked her head to the side nearly landing her on the ground. Her cheek burned like fire, and she spat out blood.

"Uncle, don't hurt her," Gill yelled and lunged for the gun.

Sanchez tried to shove him aside, but Gill was too muscular. He grabbed the hand holding the gun and twisted it. Sanchez cursed, wrapped his other arm around his neck, and squeezed.

Lily backed away, fearing the gum might go off. Gill's face darkened into a deep purple.

"Stop, you're hurting him!" she screamed. Hoping to break his grip, she grabbed his arm and began yanking on it.

The governor's elbow jerked and struck her in the jaw, sending her sprawling. Flashes of red and orange blinded her.

While she tried to clear her head, the two men fell to the driveway and continued to struggle. Gill broke loose from his uncle's grip. He struck him in the nose with his palm.

Blood spurted.

He spat out a string of expletives and lunged for Gill's throat.

Gill threw his arms up knocking the gun from his uncle's hand. It clattered to the concrete. Both men dove for it like it was a loose football.

An explosion shattered the night as the weapon discharged.

Heat whizzed past Lily's head striking the car window. Sharp fragments of glass zinged in all directions. She screamed and grabbed her arm. Blood seeped between her trembling fingers.

"Run!" Gill yelled.

Lily forced her mind to clear and her legs to work. She sprinted over a cattle-gate and across an open field.

Another shot echoed through the crisp air, and bile crept up her throat. "Oh Lord, don't let it be Gill," she prayed.

Gulping air, she staggered into a stand of trees. As she pushed deeper, angry thorns ripped at her blouse, snagging her exposed flesh. A zipper of crimson formed on her arm and began to spread. The urge to scream was palpable, but she clamped her hand over her mouth and hunkered down into a tight ball.

Two headlights appeared at the far end of the field. The roar of the four-wheeler, driven by Sanchez grew in intensity. The ground shook as he circled the stand of trees trying to locate Lily.

Blindly, he fired a shot. The bullet struck the tree next to her sending bark cascading over her. She let out a muffled scream.

"Hold it right there." It was Gill. He stood in the glare of the four-wheeler's headlights, his arms extended.

"Don't make me do this, Willie, step aside," the governor hollered over the roar of the four-wheeler.

Willie shifted his position. "No, I won't let you kill my sister."

Crazed laughter echoed through the night air. The governor had completely lost control of his senses, and was insane with rage. "Get out of the way you fool or I'll shoot you where you stand."

"No, Uncle, I've listened to you too long. No more killing, no more hiding. It's time I faced who I am."

"And who are you, Willie," he sneered, "the son of a prostitute, a filthy—"

A shot rang out stopping his tirade mid-sentence.

Sanchez groaned and staggered. Knees buckling, he tumbled forward and dropped his gun. Shock registered on his face as he touched the gaping hole in his chest. His hand came away stained dark with blood. The bullet which passed through Sanchez's body, struck Gill in the arm, spinning him around. He lost his balance and fell.

"Uncle," Gill sputtered and crawled next to the dying man.

Quivering from shock, the older man raised his head

to speak. "I'm sorry, Willie." He coughed and a trickle of blood coursed down his chin. "For everything." His hand reached out as if trying to grasp something. Then it relaxed and dropped to the ground with a soft thud.

Chapter Forty-Four

Earlier that evening, Nelson Peterson parked his car on the other side of the creek and had taken a position on a small ridge.

Having overhead Gill and Lily's conversation, he knew they were going to his uncle's ranch. He also knew there was one last photograph he needed to collect … the one with Lily, Sanchez, and Gill.

No one was allowed to take a picture of his girl. No one.

It was Sanchez's fault. He insisted on it and now he was going to pay for his mistake. Peterson cursed himself for missing his target the first time. The bullet accidentally missed and struck some bystanders. For that, he was deeply sorry. As a physician, he was sworn to heal, to give life, not take it. But in certain circumstances, it had to be done.

This was one of those circumstances. He'd already formed a plan. From his position on the other side of the creek, he could clearly see the governor's house. One shot, that's all it would take, and he would be rid of the last obstacle between him and Lily.

However, circumstances had changed with the entrance of Gill. As long as Gill stood in the way, there was little chance she would love him completely. Who knows, Gill might have taken a picture of her with his phone.

That was not permitted.

Gill had to die.

As he watched the scene unfold, a cruel smile spread across his face. One shot, that's all it would take and Lily would see he means her no harm. One shot and all her troubles would be over, and they could be united … at last.

In the gathering shadows, he watched Sanchez ride a four-wheeler across the meadow with Gill trailing after him. It provided the perfect cover for him to reposition himself. Over the roar of the four-wheeler and the shouting, he crept close enough to be within a few hundred yards.

After seeing Sanchez fire his gun at Lily, Peterson knew what he had to do. He had to save her. He had to save the woman of his dreams; his lover, his wife.

As the shouting continued, he took aim.

Sanchez stepped off the four-wheeler and moved into its headlights. Gill stood, his arms outstretched. Lily was somewhere in the thicket.

One shot.

He inhaled and let it out slowly, just as he practiced hundreds of times.

Squeeze the trigger slowly.

Steady, stay focused.

Aim for the chest.

The weapon exploded, shattering the night. Sanchez's steps faltered. He stumbled forward with the force of the bullet.

One shot, one bullet, two kills.

He was proud of his skill.

These hands can kill or bring life. Tonight, they will do both.

Dropping the rifle in the creek as he crossed the wooden bridge, he emerged from his hiding place. He ignored the two bodies lying side by side and pushed into the thicket where he found Lily curled in a fetal position.

***

"Lily?"

She heard her name, but the voice wasn't Gill's. It wasn't her brother's.

"Dr. Peterson?" His name caught in her throat. She felt the world tilt.

"Yes, it's me. I've come to save you.

"But how? Why?"

He moved a step closer. Kneeling down, he spoke in a tender voice. "Don't you know by now? I love you. I've come to claim you as my bride."

The memory of him hovering over her that day in the honeymoon suite turned her stomach, and she retched.

She wiped her mouth with the back of her hand. "I don't want you to save me. I don't love you and I never will." The words gushed out before she could stop them.

He looked hurt.

"I'm sorry. I didn't mean that to sound so harsh, but it's true."

"That doesn't matter," he said, his tone raspy. "One day you will. Now come with me. I have a car waiting and a future destiny to fulfill."

Before she could stop him, he grasped her wrist and pulled her to her feet. It wasn't done in anger, but forceful enough to cause her to stumble. He scooped her in his arms and began to carry her across the field toward the wooden bridge.

"Stop right there!"

Chapter Forty-Five

Using the phone locator app on my phone, I tracked Lily's movements throughout the day.

When she headed in the direction of Sanchez's ranch, I knew she was in trouble. And when my phone pinged number One, meaning emergency, my heart rate skyrocketed.

Pushing my rented car to the limit, I raced up the graveled road leading to the governor's ranch. When I arrived, I found the governor's limo sitting next to Gill's Jeep. Its engine was still hot and I knew he had gotten there only minutes before me.

Weapon drawn, I entered the governor's residence with Wag close at my heels. I swept the downstairs looking for movement but found none. Finally, we moved to the den.

My blood turned to ice as my eyes found the picture of Gill and Governor Sanchez and Lily.

"This explains a lot—"

A gunshot shattered my thoughts, sending my heart into overdrive. It was all I could do to keep a grip on Wag's tether and the butt of my weapon as he tugged forward. With care, I moved as quickly as my training would allow. The rest of the house was unoccupied, so I followed the raised voices outside. Holding me gun held at shoulder height, I swept the area.

In the distance, a pair of orange beams bounced over the rough terrain heading for a small stand of trees. A lone figure stumbled along several yards behind it.

In the moonlight, I watched the staggering figure stop between the orange headlights and the trees.

"It looks like Gill," I whispered.

Following more slowly, Wag and I crept along, keeping a low profile.

A crisp shot rang out, and I ducked. After a beat, I lifted my head. Two men lay strewn across the ground. One was crawling toward the other. Further ahead, a man appeared at the far end of the field and raced toward the stand of trees.

I heard voices and froze. Lily was pleading with someone. He was not listening.

Still in a low crawl, I closed the distance just as the man emerged from the shadows carrying Lily in his arms.

It was Dr. Peterson, and he had Lily.

Leveling my gun, I yelled, "Stop right there!"

Dr. Peterson froze and peered into the darkness. Apparently, he hadn't seen me until I was nearly upon him.

"Let her go." Despite my injuries, my hand was steady, my voice firm. Wag strained at his leash, but I held him back not knowing if he had a gun or not.

"I don't think so, Mr. O'Reilly." Peterson's tone was etched with sarcasm. "I'm afraid my rendezvous with Lily is past overdue. Now lower your weapon and we'll be on our way."

Lily squirmed, glaring at him with fire in her eyes.

"I took a step closer. He countered by yanking Gill to his feet. The bullet he'd fired must have passed through Sanchez's body and struck Gill in the arm. He was wounded and bleeding, but not seriously.

Clutching him around the throat, Peterson backed toward the bridge.

Wag and I followed, keeping our distance.

Gun held level.

I knew I couldn't make the shot. Peterson kept Lily's body between himself and me.

Once he'd reached the bridge, he slung Gill over the railing, and held him by his belt.

Beneath the wooden bridge, raged an angry set of rapids and falls. Even from this distance, I could hear the thunderous pounding of the river as it cascaded over the precipice.

"Time to decide, Mr. O'Reilly, your daughter or your son."

Above Lily's pleadings for him to pull Gill back, all those questions about what I would do for a righteous cause became crystal clear. Even though he was unarmed, he was a threat to my family ... to those I loved. I had one shot. I wouldn't miss.

"If you shoot me, Gill dies."

His words turned my finger to ice. I couldn't squeeze the trigger if I tried.

I couldn't do it.

"Oh, Lord, help us!" My whispered prayer had no sooner escaped my lips when Gill's good arm appeared above the railing. Like a python, it curled around Peterson's waist and pulled.

Peterson dropped Lily trying to steady himself, but Gill's grip was too strong, his weight too much and the two of them toppled over the railing and plunged into the icy current.

In an instant, they were gone.

***

I raced to Lily's side. Her wild eyes stared into the white foam rushing beneath our feet.

Grasping the edge of the railing, she plunged over the edge before I could stop her.

"Lily." My voice was swallowed up in the night.

Retracing my steps, Wag and I began to run along the edge of the river, calling Lily's name. The further we ran, the louder the pounding surf became, and I knew, if I didn't do something, I'd lose my family.

***

Moonlight reflected off the churning whitewater.

Lily's head bobbed along the current as she struggled to stay afloat.

Not far ahead, she could see Gill and Mr. Peterson locked in battle. Despite the dangerous outcroppings and fallen logs, the two men grappled with each other.

Kicking against a rock, Lily launched herself faster, trying to catch up with her brother. She could hear the two men cursing as one would shove the other's head under the foaming tide.

Slick with moisture and moss, a large boulder divided

the river. To one side was a whirlpool sucking everything into its vortex, to the other side, a thirty-foot drop.

"Gill, watch out," Lily's cries were barely audible.

At the last second, he released his grip on Peterson. The man's head struck the boulder, knocking him unconscious. His limp body got caught in the rapids and tumbled over the falls where jagged rocks waited.

Gill braced himself against the boulder fighting the surge, which threatened to suck him into the whirlpool. If he lost his grip, he would be sucked under.

Before she could stop, Lily slammed into him. He caught her before she plunged over the edge. Gripping each other, they clung to a boulder. With his injury, his good hand began to weaken. It was only a matter of time before they were swept away.

***

From the river bank, I watched in horror.

I'd seen Peterson go over the falls. Now, as Lily and Gill's grasp weakened, the force of the current threatened to carry them to their deaths. All I could see was my family being washed away over the edge of the falls. Seeing the two young people clinging for life in the midst of the raging river, broke my heart.

I tried calling to them, but the noise from the falls sucked my voice away. And in the darkness, they couldn't see me anyway. Releasing my grip on Wag's leash, I knelt on one knee and prayed that God would intervene.

Before I could grab his leash, Wag plunged into the

river and began to swim to their rescue. His powerful legs kicked wildly as he made steady progress against the tide.

Peering into the darkness, I held my breath. As if God spoke, the clouds moved aside and a golden beam, like a spotlight illuminated the place where Lily and Gill clung. Wag homed in on their position and Gill reached out and grabbed his leash. Once he was secure, Wag began to pull them to safety, but as his legs tired, the current began to sweep them dangerously close to the falls. I knew within a few seconds they would be gone and with them, my whole life.

Without hesitation, I kicked off my boots and dove into the current. Two powerful strokes and I was within inches of Lily's hand. My fingers closed around her wrist, and I began to swim toward the shore.

The progress was slow. Pulling two adults and a dog required my all.

And I did.

After one final burst of energy, I grabbed a limb with my free hand. Wag dragged Gill to the shore and began to shake himself. As he did, he pelted me with icy droplets of water, but it didn't matter.

We had saved my family.

Afterword

❝How did you figure it out?" Lily asked from her perch on the corner of the Loveseat occupied by Troy Ashcroft.

I roused, dragged my eyes away from the fireplace and blinked. It took a while for my head to clear. After all that had transpired, I was barely able to form a cogent thought.

Lily watched me expectantly. She'd recovered from her ordeal rather quickly and was fawning over Gill and me like a mother hen.

Wag took his position next to me on the couch and laid his head on my lap. Running my fingers through his thick coat, I patted him gently.

Willie, who refused to be called Gill any longer, sat with his arm bandaged in my favorite chair, but it didn't matter.

"Yeah, Trace," Cami prodded. "Time to tell all."

The hours since our return home had been filled with a trip to the hospital to get Willie stitched up, and a visit to the police department to report the deaths of Governor Sanchez and Nelson Peterson.

To my surprise, the chief took the time to actually congratulate me for my efforts in solving a missing person's case involving a child … my child.

By the time we'd returned home, I was beat, but Lily's question couldn't wait.

"I checked Willie's dorm room for fingerprints and matched them with the set we recovered from the dump truck. They also matched the ones we found on the murder weapon."

Willie let out a painful groan. "What an idiot."

"Don't worry. Lily vouched for you. All the charges against you have been dropped. Plus, you were mentally and emotionally abused by the governor, so that played in your favor."

Lily stood in front of the fireplace, wrapped her arms around her waist. "But how did you know we were at the governor's ranch? I didn't tell anyone."

Holding my phone with the locator app, I smiled.

Recognition registered on her face. "Pretty sneaky. I'm glad you were watching my back."

I cast a glance in Troy's direction. "Actually, it was his idea."

Lily offered him a sheepish smile. "I'm sorry for the way I treated you. I was just so—"

He stood and silenced her with his finger on her lips. "We can talk about this later. I'm just relieved it's all over."

His statement was interrupted by someone knocking on our front door.

"Who could that be?" I sent Troy an anxious look.

He fingered his service weapon and followed me to the door.

After unlocking the deadbolts, I took one last look

through the peephole and swung the door open.

"Mr. Carnes."

He stood bolt straight, a white cloth rested comfortably on his right forearm, which held a silver tray. He gave me a curt bow and extended the tray in my direction.

"Sir, I believe this pertains to you." a slight smile tugged at the corners of his mouth.

I pulled my eyes from his benevolent gaze and noticed what it was he was offering me. It was the jewelry box.

I lifted it carefully.

The elderly man teetered a moment, then caught himself. "Sir, may I come in?"

I stepped back.

Lily was already on her feet. "Grandpa," she blurted and gathered him into a warm embrace.

His eyes welled and tears ran down his rugged cheeks.

"Good to see you again, my Dear," his voice wavered.

"Come in, let me introduce you to the rest of my family," Lily said as she guided him to the living room.

I followed.

After the introductions were made, Carnes nodded.

"Open it," his tone warm, his eyes dancing with an inner glee. It was as if he knew what secrets the jewelry box held.

Lily tugged the necklace from around her neck. The key baring the letter 'L' tangled freely from its golden chain.

"Hey, I have one of those," Willie said. With his good hand, he worked a similar golden necklace out from under his shirt. Similar in every way with the exception of one thing, it bore the letter 'W.'

Placing the two sides together, they formed the complete key. All that was needed was for Lily to insert it into its slot to unlock the secret which had long eluded. Fingers trembling, she slid the key into the slot. A soft click followed and a secret compartment popped open. By now, all eyes were riveted on the box.

"What is it?" Willie asked, his excitement radiated throughout the room.

Carefully, Lily slid the drawer out revealing a single sheet of paper. Fingers trembling, she lifted it. It was a note from Rose Beretta and it was notarized.

Eyes scanning the scrawl, she read,

> I, Rose Beretta, being of sound mind and purpose, do hereby bequeath the property of the Beretta estate with all its holdings to Trace O'Reilly and to his heirs. The suite occupied by my good friend, Carnes Bradbury will remain in his possession as long as he chooses to enjoy it.
>
> Signed, Rose Beretta

We stared at one another, not speaking.

Finally, Lily broke the silence. "Grandpa Carnes, I mean Grandpa Bradbury, did you know about this?"

The corners of his mouth stretched into a broad grin. "Yes, my dear. You see, the estate was never owned by Luciano or his wicked son. It was always Mrs. Beretta's.

She had her will altered after Mr. O'Reilly was exonerated sighting her high regard for your integrity."

I felt my face warming.

"And then there is the matter of this," he continued. Pulling an envelope from his inner coat pocket, he offered it to Willie.

Mouth gaping, Willie stared at it. "What is it?"

"Open it and you will find out." Carnes said softly.

With a slight tremble in his fingers, Willie took the proffered envelope and slid open the flap. He gave us a quick glance before pulling out a crisp official looking document. It read; William O'Reilly, born 11:30 p.m., April 4, 1992 in Sacramento Hospital.

"Hey, that's the same day I was born," Lily said, leaning over to catch a glimpse of the document.

Willie pulled another document from the envelope and staggered. Tears stung his eyes, and he handed it to me. "I can't read it."

I took the document from his shaky fingers and read, "Guillermo Jose Miguel Tampico, born 10:30 p.m., April 4, 1992. Deceased 11:00 p.m. April 4, 1992."

Father O'Leary's signature was clearly visible.

"So that explains a lot. Sanchez was willing to kill Monica, Father O'Leary, Rosa and even Antonio to keep these certificates from coming to light."

"Yes, and apparently Jimmy wanted a piece of the action," Troy added. He tried to blackmail the governor and it got him killed."

As Cami, Troy, Lily and I gathered around Mr. Carnes, Lily tugged Willie into the midst of the group. "Daddy, as you know, Willie saved my life. I think it's time we help him get his life back."

Cami wrapped her arms around me as I pulled my children into a group hug. I placed a kiss on her forehead.

"Honey, it's time we all got our lives back."